Praise for S.C. Stephens

"From page one, this book is impossible to put down."

—Abbi Glines, on *Thoughtless*

"S.C. Stephens at her best!"

—Katy Evans, on *Thoughtful*

"Addicting and heart pounding—you won't be able to put it down until you've devoured every word."

—Christina Lauren, on *Untamed*

SOMETHING LIKE PERFECT

ALSO BY S.C. STEPHENS

Thoughtless Series

Thoughtless
Effortless (Book 2)
Reckless (Book 3)
Thoughtful (Thoughtless alternate POV)
Untamed (Book 4)

Rush Series

Furious Rush
Dangerous Rush (Book 2)
Undeniable Rush (Book 3)

Conversion Series

Conversion
Bloodlines (Book 2)
'Til Death (Book 3)
The Next Generation (Book 4)
The Beast Within (Book 5)
Family Is Forever (Book 6)

Stand-Alone Books

Collision Course
It's All Relative
Under the Northern Lights

SOMETHING LIKE PERFECT

S.C. STEPHENS

This is a work of fiction. Names, characters, organizations, places, events, and incidents are either products of the author's imagination or are used fictitiously.

Published by Montlake, Seattle

www.apub.com

ISBN-13: 9781542003810
ISBN-10: 1542003814

Cover design by Caroline Teagle Johnson

Printed in the United States of America

For KK. Thank you for keeping me moving forward!

Chapter One

It was a chilly night in LA, and I wrapped my jacket tighter around myself as my friends and I walked down the sidewalk to our favorite club. I was exhausted, and I really wanted to go home to my apartment and sleep for about a hundred years, but I couldn't. Today was my best friend's birthday, and we were celebrating.

"Valerie, why do you look like you're about to pass out?"

I looked over at the tall redhead walking beside me. Stephanie, the birthday girl and my best friend. "Culinary school is kicking my ass," I told her. She frowned, like she was worried about me, and I quickly swished my hand to wipe away her concern. "It's a good tired, I swear. I love school." Even as I said it, visions of soufflés, risottos, and tartars filled my head. God, I couldn't wait for Monday.

Smiling, her blue eyes shining with joy, Steph looped her arm around mine. "Well, I'm glad you're coming out with us. And not just because it's my birthday. You need to unwind." Steph had always been the protector of our little group, caring and empathetic. She was the one we all went to when we needed a shoulder to cry on.

I grinned at Steph, and the smile instantly turned into a yawn. On the other side of me, my friend Alicia smacked my arm. "Stop that. You're making me tired, and it's not even ten o'clock." Her dark eyes sparkled with mischief as she smirked at me. Where Steph was sweet, Alicia was blunt and outspoken. She told the world exactly what she felt about it; I loved that about her.

"Sorry," I said, clenching my jaw to stop myself from yawning again.

My third friend, Chloe—walking behind me with my sister, Kylie—started giggling. Cute, sweet, and so short you could almost tuck her in your pocket, Chloe was the official jokester of the group; she found everything funny and had a way of making everyone else see the humor in any situation.

At hearing Chloe snort, Kylie started laughing too. I tossed a glare at her. The sister code clearly stated that she shouldn't laugh at my misery. Kylie cringed in apology, then continued laughing. So much for the sister code.

Rolling my eyes, I twisted back around to face the club that was now just a few feet away. The thumping music inside the building was so loud I could feel it vibrating through my chest. Its energy perked me up a bit. Maybe Steph was right. Maybe this was exactly what I needed.

The five of us walked inside and headed straight for the bar. Dancing was always better once you had a shot or two dulling your senses. I ordered a round of whiskey for everyone, then passed them out.

After everyone had one, we formed a circle—a symbol of our impenetrable bond. "To Steph," I said. "The best one of us."

"I don't know about that," Alicia quipped, fluffing her dark wavy hair. "I'm pretty fabulous."

We all laughed, then clinked our glasses together. "To Steph," we all said as one, and then we tipped the glasses back. It burned in the best possible way, and I was immediately back at the bar, ordering another round. This night was going to be so expensive but so worth it.

Kylie joined me at the bar while I waited for the bartender to precisely fill each shot glass. My sister was chewing on her lip, looking really guilty about something, so I couldn't help but ask her what was going on. "You okay?"

She grinned as she tucked her long blonde hair behind her ears. "Yeah, why?"

"I don't know. You just seem like you want to say something, but at the same time, you don't want to say something."

With a groan, she dropped her head back. "Ugh, I hate how you can read me like a book."

Half smiling, I shrugged. "That comes with being a big sister."

She raised a pale eyebrow, amused. "You're ten months older than me. That hardly qualifies you as being wiser than me."

My smile grew as I grabbed some of the finished drinks. "All that matters is the older part. Doesn't matter if it's ten months or ten minutes. I'll always know best."

She laughed at my statement, then bit her lip again. "Okay . . . I have a secret."

Handing her two of the glasses, I let out a loud groan. "Oh my God, Kylie . . . how many times have I told you the first step to spilling a secret is telling someone you have one? Seal those lips."

She giggled again, then shook her head. "Oh, I'm not spilling anything yet."

"Then why did you tell me? Are you trying to drive me insane?"

"No, I'm just . . . I'm excited." She immediately held a hand up, like she was blocking my questions. "But it's too soon to say anything. I don't want to jinx it. You'll know soon, though, I promise."

I studied her face for a moment. The big bright-blue eyes, almost carbon copies of mine. The commercial-worthy silky blonde hair, also similar to mine. We definitely had a familial resemblance, but Kylie had inherited Mom's perky nose and perfect cheekbones, while I'd inherited Dad's height—I had a good six inches on her. Curiosity was killing me, but my sister was an integral part of my life, closer than a best friend, so I respected her wishes.

"All right, fine, keep your secret. But if you don't spill soon, I will hold you down and tickle your armpits until you tell me everything inside your head. *All* your secrets will be mine."

Her mouth dropped open as she gaped at me. "You wouldn't dare."

"Oh yes, I would. Just you remember that."

She smirked, then laughed, then nodded. "I'll tell you everything soon, I swear. And like your schooling, it's a good thing, Val. A great thing."

Her eyes were sparkling so much I could practically see the heart bubbles floating in the air around her. Carefully wrapping my arm around her in a quick hug, I indicated where the other girls were waiting. "Enough sappy stuff. Let's get our drink on."

"Yes, ma'am," she said, laughing. Then she helped me carry the alcohol to our friends.

Two hours later, I was higher than a kite and feeling no pain. I'd definitely overdone the celebrating, but I had really needed the break. I hadn't expected training for my dream career to be as intense and high pressure as it was. My teacher believed in realism, and his classroom was more like a battlefield than a kitchen. But he didn't want to coddle us when he knew the real world would be vicious. He wanted to give us a taste so we could drop out now if we didn't like it. I appreciated that. I'd rather know exactly what I was getting into than think I was getting something else and be caught off guard. After completing this school, I would be ready for anything. *Bring it, world. I'm ready.*

By the time we were done for the night, my head was twirling like a top. Steph patted my back the entire cab ride home. "Are you sure you don't want me to stay overnight with you? I really don't mind."

Withholding a groan as I sat with my head down between my legs, I shook my head. "No, I'm fine. I just . . . need sleep." And the world to stop spinning.

Steph still saw me into my apartment and tucked me into bed before leaving. That was just the sort of friend she was. It made me feel guilty. It was her birthday; I should be holding *her* hair back while *she* emptied her stomach, not the other way around.

~

When I woke up in the morning, I regretted every life decision I'd ever made. My head was throbbing, my stomach was roiling, and I was still wearing the same clothes I'd had on last night. Coffee. I needed coffee. But not the lame, watered-down version I made on my kitchen counter. No, I needed full-strength, no-messing-around, made-by-a-professional espresso. Good thing my favorite coffee bar was right around the corner from my apartment. Thank God for city living.

After clearing my stomach—three times—I changed my clothes, snatched my purse, grabbed my sunglasses, and made my way to the caffeine haven. The smell instantly soothed my churning stomach when I stepped inside. I was halfway to feeling better. One cup of joe, and I'd be nearly human again.

I felt like death as I waited for my turn. Why did getting coffee take so long? *Pour, next. Pour, next.* It seemed like it should take no time at all to get through the line. But then again . . . you couldn't rush perfection, and these guys really did make the best coffee in the city.

At least I had something yummy to look at while I waited. The man in front of me had to be a full-time model. If he did anything other than promote underwear for Calvin Klein, I'd be shocked. His body was perfect—not too bulky, not too lean, and clearly defined. He couldn't hide that with his shirt and shorts. And the glimpses I'd caught of his face had only confirmed my model theory—perfect cheekbones, masculine jaw, green freaking eyes. And to top it all off, he had perfect semishaggy, *I don't care, but I really care* light-brown hair. He was the epitome of every woman's fantasy, and I was too sick to my stomach to make a move on him.

Why did I have to run into him today? I knew I looked awful, I knew my hair was atrocious, and I knew that underneath my gargantuan sunglasses, my eyes were worn and bloodshot. Looking like this was *not* how you grabbed the attention of a guy like that. It killed me that I'd never see him again after today, and as I stepped up to the barista, I prayed that somehow I'd be given an opportunity to interact with him. Something that would trump how I looked today.

"How much do I owe you?" I croaked, my voice unusually raspy.

"Nothing. The man in front of you paid."

My eyes shot wide open at that, and I lowered my sunglasses to look at her. "What?" *Because I swear you just said that hot guy bought me coffee.*

The barista pointed at said stranger. Her eyes looked a little starry as she stared at him. "He paid for your drink."

Mouth agape, I looked over at him. He was busy talking to someone in the waiting area, not looking my way. As I got a good look at his face, instead of just quick profile glances when he'd turned his head, my heart started racing. Wow . . . this was the most attractive man I'd ever seen, and he'd just bought me a drink. Sure, it was only coffee, but . . . that had to mean something, right? He'd noticed me, and he was interested?

Play it cool; don't overreact. I didn't want to scare him away by being overeager. Or by being really hungover. Why hadn't I showered this morning? Or brushed my teeth?

I was nervous as I moved into the waiting area. Why did this have to happen today? When I didn't have my battle armor on, when all my defenses were down? I hadn't believed in the power of makeup before, but I sure did now. A guy this gorgeous . . . well, you'd better look like Megan Fox to approach him. And I didn't at the moment. But he'd bought my coffee. Not acknowledging him would be rude, so I had no choice but to approach him. Just to thank him, of course.

Nervous thrills tore through my veins as I stepped closer to him. They intensified when the man he was talking to picked up his coffee, leaving him alone. *Now's my chance.* I inched into his personal space, and he turned his attention in my direction. Once those jade eyes focused in on me, my breath caught, and I swear my heart stopped. How did so much perfection end up in one person?

Knowing I should stop staring and say something, I quickly blurted out, "Thank you." He tilted his head, confused, and I indicated the baristas making espressos behind me. "For the coffee. Thank you for the coffee."

He glanced back at them, then returned his attention to me . . . and smiled. "You're welcome. I try to pay it forward whenever I can, and it seemed like you could really use a pick-me-up today."

A small part of me was disappointed by his answer—he wasn't hitting on me; I'd just been the lucky recipient of a kind gesture—but mostly I was awed by his sweetness. Hot *and* generous. And no wedding ring. How was this man not married yet?

As I mumbled an incoherent response, his eyes flicked over my appearance, and his smile slowly shifted into an adorable smirk. "Rough night last night?" he asked, playfulness in his voice.

Exhaling a heavy breath, I nodded. Then I lowered my sunglasses and let him see my tired eyes. "You have no idea."

He laughed, and I had to restrain myself from grabbing my phone and recording the sound so I could listen to it over and over again. He hadn't run away yet, and he'd even extended the conversation. Maybe the coffee had been an act of kindness and not flirtatiousness, but that didn't rule out the possibility that he was interested. His eyes were certainly warm and friendly. Receptive. I had nothing to lose and a *lot* to gain, so I sucked in a deep breath and took a chance.

"Maybe I could repay your kindness with a drink tonight? Maybe dinner too . . ."

My heart rampaged inside my chest as I waited for a response from him. His smile widened, and my chest almost burst, there was so much hope running through it—*he's going to say yes.* But then he frowned, turning the bright hope into icy disappointment. "Sorry, I can't. I just started seeing someone. It's new, but I really like her."

I blew out a long exhale. Of course he was seeing someone. Hot men didn't stay single for long. Especially when they were sweet. Especially when they clearly had good hearts. Because it would have been really easy for him to say he was single and date us both for a while. But he hadn't. He'd fessed up immediately. And now I was pretty sure I was in love with him.

Trying to hold in my embarrassment at being rejected, I slapped on a smile and told him, "No problem. Thank you for the coffee." It was at this point that I noticed something about him that I really should have noticed earlier. "Oh, wow . . . your shirt . . . I have the *exact* same one. That's my favorite show."

He looked down at the shirt I couldn't stop staring at. It was an image from a really obscure anime show that I loved. A show I adored completely on my own, because everyone I knew either hated it or had never heard of it and had no interest in learning more about it. And here he was, displaying his fondness for it on his chest.

"Oh yeah?" he said, looking back up at me. "I rarely meet anyone who knows what this is. Except at anime conventions, of course. Then I get showered with compliments and high fives." He laughed and shrugged, and I was completely blown away. He went to conventions. He loved anime. He loved *my* anime. Now I *knew* I was in love with him.

"I know what you mean," I murmured. "I go every year, and I always wear my shirt." *Our* shirt.

His eyes sparkled as he tilted his head at me. "Huh. Small world, isn't it?"

Yes. And no. If the world were just a bit smaller, I would have met him when he was single.

The barista suddenly called out the name Jake, and this truly captivating stranger swiveled his head her way. Jake. *Thank you, barista.* Now I had a name for my fantasies.

Jake turned his head back to me, then stuck out his hand. "That's me. It was nice to meet you . . ."

He let the sentence trail off with an eyebrow raised. Knowing what he wanted, I said, "Valerie," then took his offered hand. Touching him sent an unexpected rush of electrified energy through me; I doubted I even needed the coffee now. His skin was the perfect mixture of rough and soft, warm and dry, firm and tender. Being connected to him was intoxicating, and I kind of never wanted to let go.

"Valerie . . ." He smiled as he slowly said my name, like he was savoring it. "Enjoy your coffee. And I hope you feel better after drinking it."

"Thanks . . ."

Our hands released, and I contained a sigh. I had truly enjoyed touching him, and I couldn't help but stare at him the entire time he picked up his coffee from the barista. Once he had it, he twisted to me, raised his cup in a cute farewell, and then proceeded to leave the café. My eyes followed him until he was gone, and then I let out the sigh I'd been holding. When I turned back to the barista, I saw that she was still staring after him, and her face looked just as forlorn as mine.

When she finally snapped out of it, she looked over at me, then made a fanning motion with her hand while mouthing, "Oh my God." I laughed as I nodded an agreement with her assessment. Yes, that man was definitely hot. And sweet, interesting . . . perfect for me. And taken. But at least he'd managed to completely turn my day around. My head no longer hurt, and my stomach no longer ached. I almost felt normal again, and I was positive I would feel amazing once I drank his thoughtful coffee.

Chapter Two

All that next week Jake was on my mind. Those emerald eyes, those sensual lips, the perfectly messy hair . . . the T-shirt that I had an exact copy of in my closet. I couldn't believe fate had thrown such a perfect specimen into my lap, only to tease me by making him unavailable. So unfair. He *had* said that he'd only just started seeing this girl, though. Maybe they wouldn't make it. Maybe they were on the verge of breaking up. But since I hadn't given him my number—and he probably wouldn't have taken it anyway—it didn't really matter if they did break it off. I had no way to contact him. Except stalk the coffee shop. Which I did. Stephanie thought I was insane when I told her what I was doing, but she hadn't seen him. If she had, she'd be scoping out the café every day with me.

"Hey there. The usual?" I nodded at the barista. She was the one who'd been drooling over Jake the day I'd met him. "One drip coffee coming up," she said, shaking her head and smiling.

"What?" I asked, paying her with the scant amount of coins I had in the bottom of my purse. Even though I always ordered the cheapest coffee on the menu, stalking Jake was turning out to be expensive. I couldn't keep this going for much longer.

"He hasn't been back," she said, taking my change.

Heat flooded my cheeks. "Who?" I asked, feigning innocence.

"You know who," she said. "Superhot, yea tall, green eyes . . . bought your coffee."

"Oh yeah . . . him. That's not why I come here," I said, nervously adjusting the strap of my purse.

She gave me a knowing grin. "Right. Because our drip coffee is *so* amazing that you couldn't possibly get it anywhere else . . . like your kitchen."

I frowned at her statement. "It's good coffee."

"It's available at the grocery store. Normally I wouldn't say something like that, but you're paying with dimes. Eventually it's going to be pennies, and I just can't handle that."

"Fine, yes," I said with a groan. "I've been waiting for him to come back. He really hasn't been in?"

She frowned, then shook her head. "Nope. It's like he was a dream. A really great dream."

I sighed, then thanked her. Guess it didn't make sense to keep returning every morning, not if this wasn't his regular java place. Then again . . . it had only been a week. A month would be a better test, if my bank account could afford it, of course. But I really needed to focus on school and forget about this guy. He was more than just a long shot; he was practically an impossibility.

~

For the next two weeks, I was fairly successful in removing Jake from my mind. I even managed to stay away from the coffee shop. My career was what mattered right now, not some dreamy yet unobtainable man. My career, my friends, and my family: those were my priorities. Which was why I was headed out to my parents' place for a family dinner. We tried to get together at least once a month, every third Sunday. Sometimes life got in the way and we had to cancel, but most months it worked out. The four of us liked hanging out together.

When I arrived at their house, I parked on the street. Even though I kind of wished someone would steal it, I locked the car before heading to my parents' door. My car was an ancient clunker from the early eighties, full of rust spots and dents. It barely ran and vibrated so badly you'd think it was falling apart, but I'd gotten it for free from a friend of my dad's, so I really couldn't complain about how run down it was. Going to school and living on my own in LA was hard enough with a good paycheck. The paycheck I earned for doing the books for my parents' carpet-cleaning business was meager at best, but the hours were incredibly flexible, and it just covered the bills. That made it a win-win.

Stepping into my childhood home, I heard my parents talking in the kitchen and turned that way. They were busy talking about their business when I entered the room and didn't notice me standing there.

"I'm just saying, maybe it's time to think about doing something else. Something more reliable. You know business has been spotty lately." Dad paused to laugh, his blue eyes mirthful. "And I don't mean that as a pun."

Mom bit her lip before responding. "But what about Valerie? She needs the job. We can't pull the rug out from under her."

Dad cracked a smile at Mom's pun while guilt flooded me. I knew exactly what they were talking about. I handled their financials, and the last three years had been rough. They'd taken a hit each year and had dipped into savings to cover themselves. I didn't like the thought that they were doing that just for me. "Hi, guys."

They both snapped their gazes my way, clearly startled to see me. I sheepishly raised a hand in greeting, then sighed. "Don't stay in a bad business for me. I can find something else. Plus, I'll eventually be done with school, and once I'm out, I'll be able to get something that will support me. And if not, then I'll get a roommate. Or three. Whatever I need to do to get by, I'll handle it. You guys don't have to worry about me anymore."

Mom sighed, then walked over and slung her arms around me. "We'll always worry about you. No matter how self-sufficient you get, that part never goes away."

"Great," I murmured, in an obviously sarcastic voice.

Mom pulled away, then smacked my arm. "Don't sass me."

I laughed at her comment, then gave Dad a quick hug before helping Mom with the salad she was making for dinner. I was always looking to practice my lightning-fast chopping skills. I was tearing through a cucumber when I heard a voice behind me say, "I'll never understand how you can do that so quickly. It defies the laws of physics."

Recognizing my sister's voice, I turned around with the knife still in my hand. I had a witty retort on my tongue, but it fell off my lips when I saw the person standing beside my sister, holding her hand and staring at me with wide, equally surprised eyes. Jake. The man I'd been wanting to see again, the man who'd been haunting my dreams, the man I was hoping would break up with his girlfriend and come find me . . . he was dating my *sister*.

Jake was just as gorgeous as that day in the coffee shop. Actually, since I wasn't suffering from a severe case of being hungover, I thought he actually looked better than I remembered. Penetrating green eyes, strong jaw, lean body, the sexiest hair I'd ever seen . . . perfection. My sister was sleeping with perfection.

My parents were clearly surprised to see Kylie with a man, so they also hadn't been informed that she was seeing someone. He must be the secret she'd hinted about at Steph's birthday party. Quite the secret.

"Kylie, you brought a friend. And this is . . . ?" Mom raised an eyebrow, waiting for an introduction.

Surprising everyone, I was the one who gave it. "Jake," I blurted out.

Mom, Dad, and Kylie all turned to me in surprise. Jake shook his head, amazement on his face. "Like I said . . . small world. It's good to see you again, Valerie."

I was a little surprised he recognized me, considering the fact that I looked so different than when we'd first met—hair washed and styled, makeup on, no sunglasses, and standing tall and comfortably, not hunched over nursing a wicked headache. "Yeah . . . small world. You're dating my sister."

Kylie frowned as she looked between us. "How do you two know each other?"

Jake lifted his hand toward me. "I briefly ran into her at a café a few weeks ago."

Kylie bunched her brows, still confused. "And you remember her name?"

Seeing my sister's wheels spinning, I eased her fears. "He was doing the pay-it-forward thing, and I was the lucky recipient. I thanked him afterward."

Kylie's face morphed into a smile. "You do that? That's so sweet."

She leaned into his side like she was melting into him. Jake grinned and wrapped an arm around her, and a sudden rush of jealousy washed through me, darkening my mood. They were so perfect together, nestled in each other's arms like that. I wanted to be happy for my sister—Jake seemed like a genuinely good person, and she deserved to be with a guy like that—but at the moment, I was too wrapped up in disappointment to be supportive. He was truly lost to me now, forever, because even if they did break up, there was no way I would hurt my sister by dating her ex.

My parents were watching the entire exchange with curious faces. Not wanting anyone to see I was upset, I disarmed the hurt in my heart and made myself say, "It's good to see you again, Jake. We're just finishing up dinner. I hope you're hungry."

He patted his stomach. "Starving."

I turned back to chopping vegetables. My mind spun while I worked; my stomach churned. How had my fantasy guy ended up being my sister's new secret boyfriend? All the images of us I'd created started shattering in my head—our first kiss, our first time, marriage, kids, growing old together. God. The fact that I already *had* all of those fake memories stored in my brain was just sad. He was a man; there were several more on the planet. I'd just have to find another one. And hope *he* was single.

Mom patted me on the back, like she somehow knew everything I was struggling with, and then she started playing hostess, offering Jake a drink before showing him where to sit at the table.

I stayed in the kitchen until the last possible moment, all the while listening to Dad carry on a conversation with Kylie and Jake. Where they'd met—a bar. How long they'd been together—a month and a half. What Jake did for a living. That question really interested me, and I leaned toward the opening into the dining room to hear his answer better.

"I'm in training to captain ships. I'm apprenticing on yachts right now, but my ultimate goal is cruise ships."

I instantly had a vision of him in a captain's uniform, and I closed my eyes to savor it. Sweet Jesus. I had to put a hand on the counter to steady myself.

Mom and I served dinner a little while later, and I couldn't stop watching Jake. Every little thing he did fascinated me. This was one obsession that was going to be difficult to shake. Maybe it would be easier if I thought of them as a couple—Jake and Kylie—like they were one person instead of two. Kake. Jylie. Something like that.

"So I heard you tell Dad you met in a bar?" I asked, looking only at my sister.

She giggled, like she was embarrassed. "Yeah, I know, it's cliché, but that's how it happened. He was alone at the bar, so I bought him a drink. We just . . . hit it off from there." She was staring at him with stars in her eyes. Was that how I'd looked when I'd stared at him at the coffee shop? I hoped not.

"That's cute . . . sweet." And fortuitous for my sister that he'd been single. That had to have been just a few weeks before the café. If she hadn't approached him that night, he would have been single when I'd approached him. And then *we'd* be holding hands under the table right now.

Jake glanced at me, and there was something in his eyes . . . a question. He had to be wondering if I'd tell Kylie about the fact that I'd asked him out. That wasn't something that I would mention, though. For one, I'd been rejected in that little scenario, although that would only strengthen Kylie's feelings for Jake if I told her that. But more importantly, I wouldn't tell her because I swore, for a second, there had been sparks between Jake and me. *I'm interested; please ask me out* sparks. And I couldn't tell my sister that I'd had a connection with her man, one that made my insides feel all gooey. No, I would keep that secret to my grave.

Redirecting his gaze to my mother, Jake politely said, "This is amazing. Best I've ever had."

Mom grinned, then shrugged and pointed at me. "I really can't take the credit. It's Valerie's recipe. She's always been the best cook in the family, and she's taught me a thing or two over the years."

I smiled at her, then raised my lasagna-laden fork. "You got the noodles perfect this time, Mom. I think you've got this one down."

Jake seemed surprised as he glanced between Mom and me. "You created this?"

The intensity of his eyes on me was almost too much. I could feel my heart rate climbing. "Yeah, I love cooking, always have."

Mom grinned brightly as she added, "She's just finishing up culinary school right now. One day she's going to have the hottest restaurant in LA, and we'll all meet there for family dinners. Assuming we can get reservations, of course."

I laughed at her comment, then shook my head. "There will always be a table reserved for you, Mom. It will have your name on it and everything."

Her eyes grew serious as she pointed her fork at me. "It better."

Jake laughed, then looked over at me with astonishment in his eyes. "That's amazing. Truly. And so is this meal. Lasagna is my absolute favorite, and I thought nobody could top my grandmother's recipe, but I think you just changed my mind. This is outstanding. When you open your restaurant, you've got to include this."

"Thank you . . ." His multiple praises had my cheeks burning with heat and my stomach swirling with glee. But then my gaze wandered to Kylie. She looked left out.

Deciding to be a good sister, I pointed her way and said, "I'm not the only talented one in the family. Kylie is pretty amazing too. I'm sure you've seen her art." Kylie had a booth at the beach, sketching caricatures for tourists. It never ceased to amaze me how fast she could accurately capture someone's essence on paper; I could barely draw stick figures. I kept trying to get Kylie to draw anime for me, but she hated the style. I couldn't help but wonder if she knew that her boyfriend was just as big a fan as I was. She was going to flip if he ever tried to drag her to a convention. And remembering that connection Jake and I shared made me a little sad.

I forcefully pushed away the feeling as Jake grinned and twisted to look at Kylie. "I have. She did one for me. It's hanging on my wall, and I'm never removing it."

Kylie looked down, like she was embarrassed. "Yeah, it's not exactly the highest form of art, but it's fun, and I get to be a little ridiculous with it, make a guy ride a shark or something. What other job allows you to do that?"

"Don't sell yourself short," Jake said. "It's amazing. You're amazing." And then he leaned over and kissed her. Watching them connect like that made something painful squeeze inside my chest. I almost felt like I was having a mini heart attack. Man, I bet he was an amazing kisser.

After dinner, Kylie went to help Mom with dessert. Dad was making himself a drink, so that left Jake and me alone together. It felt wonderful and awful to have some private time with him. "So . . . my sister," I said, tossing a playful grin his way.

Shaking his head, he looked down at the table. "Yeah . . . what are the odds?"

I looked around to make sure we were alone, then leaned in and said, "Thank you for not mentioning that I asked you out. That would be totally embarrassing."

He grinned, and then his smile softened. "Yeah, well, it wasn't exactly a shining moment for me."

I bunched my brows in confusion. He'd been a perfect gentleman about everything. "What do you mean?"

His eyes flicked around the room, also making sure it was empty. "There was a moment, a flicker of a heartbeat, where I wanted to say yes."

My eyes widened at his confession. Even with me looking like a hot mess, a part of him had wanted to go out with me. He found me attractive. He found me interesting enough to possibly date. He would have been willing . . . if he'd been single. And that made all of this a million times more painful.

Chapter Three

Jake was once again firmly stuck in my mind after that night, only now it was worse. Instead of fantasizing about our limitless potential, I had to sit on the sidelines and watch as he and my sister fell in love. I had to hear Kylie talk about their escapades—the B&B he took her to for the weekend, their late-night walks along the beach, Kylie meeting his parents and instantly bonding with them. But as the weeks turned into months and it was clear their relationship wasn't ending, I sort of got used to the painful, jealous feeling that forever lingered in my chest. It became a very familiar ache, one I was able to shove in a corner and ignore. Most of the time.

"Valerie! You did it! We're so proud of you!" Stephanie squeezed her arms around me in a crushing hug. I tried to laugh, but I couldn't breathe.

When she let me go, I let out a loud exhale. "Thanks."

Alicia beamed at me. "Culinary school graduate . . . man, I'm so excited for you to make us good shit. Now that you're not swamped, dinner is at your place every night, right?"

I lifted an eyebrow at her. "Now that I'm done with school, I need to get a job so I can start saving for a restaurant. Or . . . saving for a loan for a restaurant." I shook my head with a sigh. "I doubt I'll be making dinner at home anytime soon."

Chloe pursed her lips in thought. "Hmm . . . I heard that mom-and-pop place was hiring."

I grimaced at her suggestion. "That's a greasy spoon diner. It's a nice thought, but I was hoping for something a little more challenging than bacon and eggs."

Alicia closed her eyes. "Mmmm . . . now I want breakfast." She opened her eyes and looked around. "We should leave this place. It's dead anyway."

We all looked around with her, and I kind of had to agree. Our favorite club was a little lackluster tonight. I guess that was what happened when you finished school on a Tuesday and chose to celebrate that fact. We probably should have waited until the actual graduation ceremony this weekend to go out, but my family wanted to take me somewhere special that night, and I didn't really want to party with my parents. Or my sister and her . . . boyfriend. Too awkward. So tonight, we were partying it up, even though it was a Tuesday.

"Okay, yeah, let's head out. But not to a restaurant," I said with a cringe. "I need a break from food for a while. Let's go to a bar."

"Now you're talking," Alicia said, smacking the table.

We gathered our things, then headed outside. Instantly, I knew we'd made the right decision; it was a relief to be away from the thumping music. When the club was packed and hopping, the music was fuel for the soul, urging the body to move. But when the club was sad and empty, it was just loud.

We debated hailing a cab to get to our next destination, but across the street was our salvation—a sports bar. Perfect. Maybe there would be some football-crazed man in there who would help me forget about Jake, at least for a few hours.

I pointed to it, then grabbed Steph's hand, pulling her in that direction. The rest of the girls followed, and within minutes, we were opening the doors. Hopefully this place was a little more alive than the club, and it seemed to be from the outside—the street around it and its tiny parking lot were crammed full. When we got inside, I thought I understood why. The place was littered with TV screens, and all of them were showing various classic sports games. It was like the best of the best everywhere I looked. I wasn't a huge sports fan, but I could appreciate the awesomeness.

Unfortunately, the awesomeness meant there weren't a lot of places for a group our size to sit. Luckily there was an empty round standing table next to the bar. I wasn't thrilled to be standing all night, but then again, leaning against the table would give any man ogling me a pretty fabulous view of my backside. Man. I seriously needed a boyfriend, or at least a fling who would help me forget about . . . things.

"I'll get the first round," Steph said. She twisted to face the bar, then turned back to us. "Hey, isn't that . . . ?"

She jerked her thumb over her shoulder, and we all twisted to look. Alicia grinned when she spotted who had gotten Steph's attention. "Oh yeah, that's him, all right. Kylie's boy toy."

I immediately closed my eyes and hoped my friends were wrong. No, it couldn't be Jake. Not here, not now. Cringing, I opened my eyes and studied the man at the bar. Sure enough, it was Jake sitting there. His back was to us, but we could clearly see his face in the mirror behind the bar.

He was here, alone, at the place we'd randomly picked for celebrating. Why did fate keep tormenting me with something I couldn't have? *It's time for a new surprise. Not the same one thrown at me again and again.*

"Oh," Chloe said, pursing her lips. "While the cat's away, the mouse will play."

I frowned at her assessment of him. Jake wasn't like that. Shaking my head, I told her, "He's not *playing*. He's watching a game on TV and drinking a beer."

Chloe lifted her eyebrow at me. "At a bar, without Kylie." As if to make her point, she added, "And isn't that how they met? Him . . . alone at a bar? We should go over there and join him. Rescue him from any potential temptations."

Alicia's grin grew. "Yes, definitely."

The two of them were already starting to walk that way when I reached out and grabbed Alicia's arm. "Guys, let him be."

Alicia frowned at me as she indicated him with her hand. "He's practically your brother-in-law. It would be rude to not go over there and say hello." Her beaming grin returned, and she slipped away from me. Great. With a reluctant sigh, I moved away from the table and joined my friends.

My heart began to pound as I approached Jake, and I wasn't sure why I was getting so nervous. It wasn't like I'd never talked to him before. It wasn't like I was stepping up to him to ask him out . . . again. No, I was just saying hello—no big deal.

Jake twisted his head when he felt people directly behind him. His pale-green eyes brightened when he saw me; then his smile widened. Everything about his face said he was very happy to see me, like I'd just made his day. That look hurt my heart a bit.

"Hey, Jake," I said, ignoring the ache his perfect face always gave me.

"Valerie, hey. What are you doing here?" Before I could answer, he stood up and hugged me. My knees almost buckled, and I couldn't answer him until he let me go and took a step back.

"I, uh . . . the last day of school was today, so the girls wanted to take me out to celebrate."

I indicated my friends. Chloe and Steph waved. Alicia wriggled her fingers in greeting.

Jake waved at them, looking much more at ease than I felt. Returning his attention to me, he said, "Well, congratulations on school being over."

"Thanks. So what are you doing here?"

Jake studied me for a moment, then looked at my friends. "I was just relaxing for a bit and watching a game. You guys want to join me?"

His gaze was including all of us, but I felt like I had a spotlight shining on me. I immediately shook my head. "No, we weren't stay—"

Before I could finish my rejection, Alicia and Chloe both blurted out, "We'd love to!" My eyes widened as I watched them grab the stools on either side of him. Oh no . . . this could *not* happen. I could not casually hang out with Jake. I could not drink myself into oblivion with Jake. I could not *relax* around him.

I smiled at him and my friends, then grabbed Steph's arm. "Sure . . . we're just gonna go look for an open table. Be right back."

Jake nodded, then was bombarded with questions by my eager friends. Steph frowned as I yanked her away. "You okay? You kind of look like you're about to pass out. Need some water?"

I checked to make sure we were out of earshot, then shook my head. "No, I need to leave."

"Why?" she asked, genuinely confused.

"I can't sit down and . . . chitchat with him, and I definitely can't drink with him."

"Why not? He's a nice guy, and he genuinely seems to like you." She looked over her shoulder at Jake and the others. Jake had taken his seat at the bar, and both Alicia and Chloe were leaning toward him, so close they were almost touching him. It made me nauseous to watch the flirting.

Closing my eyes, I inhaled a deep breath. "Because he's my sister's boyfriend," I said, opening my eyes. "He's dating Kylie, so hanging out feels . . . weird."

Steph's brows bunched in confusion. "Why is hanging out with him weird? Unless . . ." Sadness suddenly morphed Steph's features as she put all the pieces together. "Oh . . . you like him, don't you?"

"No, of course not." She raised a knowing eyebrow at me, and I instantly caved. "Okay . . . maybe. But he's with Kylie, and they're . . . really happy."

"Are you sure?" she asked, glancing back toward the bar.

I couldn't look with her. "Yeah," I said, my voice morose. He liked me, sure, but he adored my sister.

Steph looked back at me with a smirk on her face. "Then why is he staring at us? Or more accurately, at you?"

I looked over to see what she was talking about. He still had his back to us, but looking in the mirror, I could see she was right. His eyes were locked on me, and it warmed me in ways I knew it shouldn't. I should definitely go home.

Steph grabbed my hand and pulled me toward a table where a group of guys was starting to leave. Pulling out a chair once they were gone, she said, "We'll just sit together for a little bit, have some drinks, and watch a game. What could possibly go wrong?"

"Right . . . ," I said, frowning. I was pretty sure that everything that had ever gone wrong in life had started with those exact words.

Steph went over to the bar to grab Jake and the girls and show them our table. Jake was the first to stand up and walk over. Alicia and Chloe seemed a little reluctant to leave their cozy side-by-side positions, but of course they followed him and joined us.

The table was a small square with only four chairs, so Jake asked a trio nearby if he could take their extra seat. They agreed, and Jake placed the chair . . . right next to me. We were so close now our elbows touched. He was *touching* me. God, this was going to be a long night.

Alicia ordered the first round—shots. I cringed when the waitress set them down. "Alicia, I don't want to get sick tonight."

She shrugged, then grabbed mine. Annoyance flashed through me, and I instantly reached over and took it back. I might not want to overdo it, but I definitely wanted to drink.

Alicia laughed . . . and so did Jake. I could feel him looking at me, so I turned my head. He lifted his little glass to mine. "Cheers," he said.

Withholding a sigh, I clinked his glass. "Cheers."

The others wanted in on it, so we all clinked glasses before tipping them back. The shot was Alicia's favorite—Fireball—and was warm and comforting going down.

"That was good," Jake said, setting it down. "I haven't had Fireball in forever."

Steph's eyes lit up at his revelation. "We need more."

I groaned as she proceeded to line up several more shots, but by the time we'd gone through them all . . . I was a lot less worried. About everything.

"More shots!" I yelled, throwing my hands into the air.

Jake laughed, his body as loose and relaxed as mine. We were as close as two people could be now, legs pressed against each other, shoulders pressed together, heads occasionally resting against the other. Lowering my hands, I let one fall on Jake's leg, the other on his arm. God, it felt good to touch him. Really good, and at the moment, I couldn't think of a reason why I *shouldn't* touch him.

Steph laughed at my comment, then shook her head. "I think you've reached your max, Val. Any more, and you'll be hurting in a way you don't want to hurt, if you know what I mean."

Having no idea what she meant, I frowned. "Come on, Steph, just one more."

She raised a fiery eyebrow at me. "That's what you said with the last one."

Alicia snorted. She'd recently gotten blonde highlights in her black hair, and they shone in the lights against her ebony skin. "She'll never learn how to self-regulate if you're always cutting her off, Steph. I say we let her pray to the porcelain god tonight."

Steph shot Alicia a glare. "And that right there is exactly why I'm her best friend."

Giggling, I leaned into Jake's side. He was so warm, so comfortable, and he smelled . . . so good.

Alicia pointed a finger at her. "Because you coddle her. She needs to stand on her own two feet. Be self-sufficient and all that."

That comment struck a nerve, even through my dulled mind. "Hey, I'm plenty self-suffic . . . ient. I just graduated, remember." My words were slurred enough to be funny, and I laughed again.

Jake grabbed my hand, and I instantly stopped laughing. All the humor had been sucked out of me, replaced with an urge to feel his lips, taste his skin. "She's right," he said. "I know my head is starting to spin, so I can only imagine how you're feeling."

Wonderful, alive . . . perfect.

His smile was so charming, so sultry, I had no choice but to agree with . . . whatever he was saying. "Yeah, okay."

His lopsided grin grew. "Great. Let's go get some cabs, then."

He pulled me to my feet as he got up, and the alcohol hit me in a rush as I stood. My vision hazed, and I sank into his side. Jake wrapped an arm around me in support, and I smiled up at him. So sweet. So undeniably sexy. So close.

Some sober part in the back of my mind wanted to add something else to that list, something . . . negative . . . but I was flying too high and feeling too good to try very hard to piece the fragmented thoughts together. All I knew right now was that I loved being near him, and I wasn't ready to let him out of my sight.

The five of us poured into the night and started walking down the sidewalk. None of us girls had driven here tonight—nobody had wanted to be the designated driver—and it seemed like Jake hadn't driven either. We were right in the thick of downtown, and cabs were constantly zipping up and down the street. We half-heartedly stuck our hands out, trying to signal one, but none of us really wanted the evening to end.

Jake and I clung to each other as we stumbled down the sidewalk. It was so wonderful to be so close to him, so connected. It felt perfectly natural, like it was always meant to be this way. Maybe we could walk all the way home. I wouldn't mind. But right then a couple of cabs pulled up beside us, dashing that dream.

Jake threw open the first taxi's door, then pulled me inside with him. Laughing, I shut the door behind me, much to the dismay of Steph, who was standing right outside the closed door, looking like she wanted inside with us. She started reaching for the door, but seeing that we were ready to go, the cab driver pulled forward onto the street, leaving Steph behind. I quickly twisted to see her very concerned eyes watching me before she climbed into the second cab.

I gave the cab driver my address, then settled into Jake's side. Excitement started churning in my belly as Jake's heat seeped into me . . . along with about a dozen warning bells. My conscience started screaming at me, reminding me that this was wrong. The alcohol flowing through my veins made me not want to listen, but when images of pressing my mouth to his flooded my brain and I began inching toward his lips, I knew I had no choice but to obey. *Too far, Val. Too far.*

I laid my head on his shoulder, both to hide my almost blunder and to keep his mouth out of view. He was just too damn tempting. He laid his head on mine, and our hands drifted together. We made the rest of the journey to my place in silence. I couldn't stop smiling, even though I felt horrible for everything that was happening.

When the cab finally turned onto my street, I felt a tiny bit more in control, and I began to worry about what Jake might be expecting from all this flirting. Would he want to come up to my apartment with me? Would he invite himself? What would I say if he did? Even though I really wanted to spend more time with him, even though I really wanted to be alone with him in my apartment, I knew we couldn't go there. I couldn't do that to Kylie. I needed to close this door before it opened any further.

Pulling back, I made myself tell him, "I had fun tonight. Thanks for hanging out with us."

He grinned as he studied me. "I had fun too. Thanks for letting me crash your party."

"Anytime," I murmured, looking down at our still-laced fingers.

Jake sighed, then pulled his hand from mine. "Guess I should let you go."

Disappointment hit me so hard my gut clenched. I did *not* want to say goodbye to him . . . but I didn't want to hurt my sister either. The silence in the cab grew loud as we inexorably approached my apartment. Jake finally broke the spell by lifting his hand and tucking a strand of hair behind my ears. The move sent shivers down my spine.

My heart rate spiked as Jake studied my face. His thumb stroked my cheek while he watched me, mesmerized. "You're so beautiful," he whispered. Then he started inching forward.

My head swam with confusion while my heart raced with anticipation. Was he really doing what I thought he was doing? It would change everything if he kissed me, and not in a good way. We'd be betraying my sister. We'd be tormenting each other. I couldn't let it go there, and yet . . . his lips were a temptation almost impossible to resist.

I could feel the desire rising within me, pulling me into him, but it was coated with a layer of self-hatred, making all of this feel very wrong. Just when our mouths were about to meet, I forced willpower to make the difficult choice for me and gently pushed him away. "Jake . . ."

He instantly snapped out of the trance he'd been in. "I'm sorry. I don't know what . . ."

"It's okay," I said, looking away.

Jake let out a heavy sigh as the cab pulled up to the curb. I could tell he felt really bad for almost kissing me. It killed me a little that he felt that way, but I also completely understood—I felt that way too. We'd gotten too close tonight. We'd crossed a line.

Still avoiding his gaze, I paid the driver my portion, then opened the door. Jake grabbed my hand before I could leave. "Valerie." I looked back at him, finally making eye contact. His green eyes were swirling with confusion. "I . . . I just . . ." After inhaling a deep breath, he let it out in a rush. "Good night."

I studied him with bunched brows, then gave him a sad smile. "Good night, Jake."

Chapter Four

I dreamed about Jake when I finally passed out. In my dream, things didn't end awkwardly. He told me I was beautiful, then leaned in to kiss me—and I didn't stop him. We shared a wonderful moment, and when it was over, I invited him up to my apartment. We talked on the couch, then kissed on the couch, then wound up in my bed. The perfect end to the perfect night. And in my dream, Jake had never met Kylie. He was single, and that was why he was alone at the bar. In my dream, there was no guilt involved with what we did. Unlike in reality, where all I felt was guilt. And sadness. Because he *had* met Kylie, and they were very much together.

As I lay in bed trying to keep my head from pounding, I absorbed that sad fact. I'd been all over him last night, and he'd been all over me. We must have looked like a couple, but we weren't. We were just two friends who had taken the flirting almost too far. Or maybe entirely too far.

Thoughts of my sister followed next. Memories of comforting her after a horrible date, telling her that she'd find someone one day and he'd be amazing because she was amazing. And that was exactly what she'd done. She'd held on to hope and kept putting herself out there, and eventually she'd found a dream boyfriend. It wasn't her fault he was also *my* dream boyfriend.

My cell phone rang as I was thick in self-pity. The shrill tone made my head feel like it was splitting in two. Who was calling me this early? Well, I supposed it wasn't early anymore. Fear shot through my veins as a thought occurred to me. It could be my sister. Oh God . . . what would I say to her? Just the thought of talking to her made me feel sick to my stomach.

Hoping it was someone else—anyone else—I dug my phone out of my bag. When I saw who it was, I let out a hefty, relieved exhale, then answered it. "Hey, Steph. How are you?"

Her voice sounded a little smug when she answered me. "I'm fine . . . how are you?"

"Regretting my life choices," I murmured.

She sniggered into the phone. "Yeah, I bet."

"It's not funny . . . but it could be so much worse. Thanks for cutting me off. And sorry about the cab thing. I didn't mean to shut you out."

"You're welcome. And don't worry about the cab, although that is kind of the reason why I called . . ."

My nose wrinkled into a cringe. "What?" I hesitantly asked.

"You and Jake . . . you guys got pretty chummy by the end of the night. I hate to be as blunt as Alicia, but I wouldn't be doing my duty as a best friend if I didn't ask . . . did you sleep with him?"

Indignation made me frown. "No, of course not. He's dating my sister, and you know I wouldn't . . ." Letting that trail off, I instead said, "And we weren't chummy. We were drunk. Thanks for that, by the way."

She laughed loudly, and I had to hold the phone away from my face to lessen the throbbing. "I wasn't pouring the alcohol down your throat. You drank it willingly. And frequently."

My stomach churned a bit as the remembered taste of Fireball flooded my mouth. I'd never be able to drink it again. "Ugh, I know." I sighed into the phone as my dilemma reared its ugly head. "Steph . . . I don't know what to do. The official graduation ceremony is Friday night, and after that, my family and me, we're all going out. I feel like it's going to be awkward now. Well, more awkward than usual."

"Why? You said nothing happened."

"Well . . . that's not exactly what I said."

"Oh my God, you *did* sleep with him," she said, gasping.

"No, I didn't, I swear. But . . . there was this moment . . ."

"What moment?" she asked, her voice cautious but curious.

A wistful sigh escaped me at the memory. "He touched my hair, he called me beautiful, and then . . . and then he leaned forward like he was going to kiss me." I heard her make a startled sound, and I quickly filled her in on what had happened next. "I didn't let him. I wanted to, but I didn't. I pushed him away, wished him good night, and got out of the cab." And dreamed about him all night long.

Steph was silent for a long time before she responded to my story. Then she let out a sad sound. "I'm so sorry, Val. Now I wish he *had* slept with you."

"What? Why?"

Her voice was soft when she answered, sympathetic. "Because then the obsession would be over. But what he did . . . that's a *fall in love with me* move."

Making my voice sound as firm as possible, I told her, "I'm not going to fall in love with him."

She didn't buy my bravado for a moment. "Val, you've been drooling over him ever since the coffee shop." My mouth popped open in surprise. "Yeah," she said. "Don't think I haven't put it together that he's the same Jake. The falling in love with him started a long time ago."

My chest squeezed with pain at her very accurate summation. "Yeah, well . . . it doesn't matter how I feel. He's with my sister, and she loves him, so that's that." Unlike in my dream, Jake wasn't a carefree single guy who'd never heard of my sister. And even if Jake and Kylie *had* broken up prior to last night, I would have pushed him away. I couldn't mess around with my sister's ex, not without having a long, brutally honest conversation with her.

"Yeah . . . that's that," Steph said, her voice even more morose than mine. "But still . . . alcohol or not . . . you two were peas in a pod, practically made for each other. I feel like that means something."

"Sure, it means I'm a horrible person."

Steph sighed into the phone. "You're not horrible. Just confused. Both of you seemed . . . confused. Maybe you should spend some time figuring it out before it . . . escalates."

Her comment made me cringe again. She was right, but still, I had no idea how to "figure out" what was going on with Jake and me. If anything actually was.

"I need to go, but thank you for checking on me, Steph."

"Of course, Val. That's what best friends do. And hey, if you ever need to call me about this, don't hesitate, okay? I'd rather you talk to me than react to something and . . . make a mistake you won't be able to take back."

Knowing just what she meant made a lump grow in my throat. I had to swallow it back before I could tell her goodbye.

~

I dwelled on what she'd said for the next few nights—and on what had happened with Jake. But then I convinced myself that my original comment on the situation had been correct—nothing had happened. We hadn't kissed, hadn't slept together. Hanging out with him and Kylie tonight would be fine. Because we were fine. All fine.

Getting ready for the ceremony helped get my mind off other aspects of my life, and I couldn't help but smile at my reflection as I smoothed out my flowing red dress. I'd done it. I'd chased my dream of pursuing my career, and now I was one step closer to my ultimate goal—my own restaurant. My life was truly starting today, and Jake . . .

he wasn't a part of that. I needed to keep that in the forefront of my mind.

Mom and Dad insisted on picking me up, so once I was ready, I waited for them. I tapped my toes while I sat on the couch, anxious for the festivities to begin. When my parents rang the doorbell, I sprang to my feet. Only it wasn't my parents at the door. It was Jake. And Kylie.

My heart soared when I saw Jake. My stomach dropped when I saw Kylie. Why were they here and not my parents? My mind swam with all of the horrible reasons why they could be at my door together. But no. Nothing had happened. We were still innocent. Or somewhat innocent.

"Hey . . . you two. What are you doing here? I thought Mom was picking me up."

Kylie grinned—not angry, then—and tossed her arms around me. "Mom's running late. She asked me to get you instead. She'll meet us there."

I frowned as we pulled apart. "I could have just driven myself. I am an adult, after all."

Jake smiled warmly at me, but there was something in his eyes. Guilt, grief . . . desire. "Mrs. Carlisle insisted you had a ride tonight. In case you wanted to . . . celebrate, I think." His eyes traveled over my dress, and I inadvertently held my breath under his inspection.

"I think I've had enough celebrating for a while," I murmured.

Kylie tilted her head as she studied me. "You too?" She jerked her thumb at Jake. "He told me that you guys ran into each other at the sports bar, but I hadn't realized you'd both tied one on that night."

I gave her a tight smile as I discreetly glanced at Jake. He looked . . . uncomfortable. From Kylie's lighthearted reaction, she didn't know specific details about that night. Like the fact that we'd been all over each other, shared a cab home, and almost kissed in the back seat of said cab. Swallowing the sudden lump in my throat, I smiled and told Kylie, "It was all Steph's fault. She seems sweet, but she's actually quite sadistic."

Kylie eyed me for a moment, then snorted. "Yeah, right."

Wanting to change the subject, I grabbed my purse and told her, "We should get going. I don't want to be late to my own graduation."

I locked up my apartment, and Kylie made an excited sound as she looped her arm around mine. "I'm so proud of you, Valerie. You did it!"

I glanced Jake's way as we began walking to the parking lot. The guilt was written all over his face. Guilt, remorse, regret—he was a walking billboard for a heavy conscience. "Yeah . . . I did it," I murmured. Or I'd almost done it. But I hadn't. And neither had Jake. He needed to snap out of his bad mood. Or else Kylie *would* get hurt.

The car ride to the school was quiet. Well, Jake and I were quiet. Kylie was chatting away, completely oblivious to the tension all around her.

When we *finally* got to the culinary school, the three of us got out of the car, then parted ways—me to meet up with the other graduates, the two of them to find a place to sit amid the audience. Nerves crawled up my spine when the actual ceremony started. Stepping out in front of a crowd was no easy task, and knowing Jake was in the crowd, watching me with those sultry green eyes, only amplified my anxiety. The ceremony itself was ridiculously corny and reminded me way too much of high school, but when they said my name, pride surged through me, blocking out my self-consciousness. Regardless of the obstacles I was facing now, I'd done it.

As I grabbed my certificate of completion from the head chef, I glanced out into the audience. I spotted my mom first—she was sobbing, just like she had at my high school graduation. Dad was sitting beside her, beaming. Kylie was sitting next to him, her smile just as wide as Dad's. And then beside her was Jake. His expression was a little unreadable. He was certainly happy for me, but there was something else there too. Something undefinable. It made my pulse quicken, made me forget I was standing on a stage in front of hundreds of strangers. Just for a split second, Jake and I were the only two people in the room. And then Kylie leaned over and kissed him, reminding me that we weren't.

I thanked the chef, then made my way off the stage. I was a little melancholy once I sat back down in my assigned seat. While I'd been eager to get through school, I'd also really enjoyed it. And for a while now, it had sort of defined me. Now that it was over, I felt a little lost. I knew that feeling wouldn't last long—eventually I'd get a job in a kitchen—but still, at the moment it felt all-consuming, and I had to dab my eyes dry more than once.

When it was all over, I walked out into the audience to find my family. Mom tossed her arms around me in a monstrous bear hug, then shoved a bouquet of flowers in my face. "We're so proud of you," she exclaimed, and she wiped her eyes. Dad gave me a similar sentiment, wrapping me in a hug too. Kylie just grinned, since we'd already hugged, and Jake just stared at me with those eyes . . . eyes that would be my undoing, I was sure.

"Should we go eat?" Dad asked. "I don't know about you, but I'm starving."

"Yeah . . . food sounds good," I told him, not really in the mood. All I could think about was Tuesday night, when Jake had had his arm over my shoulders and I'd been glued to his side. Lately, that image filled my every waking thought.

"I found the perfect place for us to go," Mom said. "It's owned by a graduate of the school. I thought that would help you feel like your dream was just within your reach."

Smiling at her sweetness, I nodded. "It does. Thanks, Mom."

I rode to the restaurant with Mom and Dad. That seemed safer. Or at least less awkward. They chatted the entire time we drove, Mom apologizing for not being able to pick me up. Apparently, her hairdresser had pushed back her appointment, screwing up Mom's entire timetable. "I've half a mind to never go back there, but . . . who am I kidding. Shelley is the only one who can handle this hair." She fluffed her long blonde locks while Dad chuckled.

A few minutes later we were stepping inside the restaurant, and I had to admit I was impressed. It was classic and stylish but fun and fresh—exactly the kind of place I wanted to open. Just being here made my creative juices start flowing, and for a moment, I forgot all about . . . what's his name.

"Oh my gosh, Mom. This place is amazing."

"I thought you might like it. Something about it screamed *Valerie* to me."

She gave me a wink, then checked us in for our reservation. We were a little early, so the hostess asked us to wait for just a few minutes while they prepared the table. I felt giddy as I took the opportunity to look around; the energy of this place was exciting every inch of me. Then I saw Jake out of the corner of my eye. He was nodding his chin toward the corner of the room, indicating he wanted me to talk to him privately. I didn't see Kylie anywhere, so I had to assume she'd gone to the bathroom or something. Even though Mom and Dad probably wouldn't think anything of it, talking to him seemed dangerous—like stepping in front of a firing squad. But still, I couldn't deny him. I was too curious.

Taking a quick look back at Mom and Dad, who were examining a menu on the wall, prepicking their meals, I stepped close to Jake. "What is it?" I asked, my heart beginning to thud in my chest. Would there ever be a time when being close to him didn't affect me? I really didn't think so.

Jake looked down as he answered me. "I just wanted . . . it's about the other night."

Nerves zinged up my spine. I didn't want to talk about the other night. I didn't want him to pop the magical bubble I'd wrapped around the evening. And I definitely didn't want to bring up the near kiss that haunted my dreams. "It's fine. There's nothing to talk about."

He glanced up at me then, an eyebrow raised as he gave me an incredulous look. "It's not fine, Valerie." Shaking his head, he let out a weary exhale. "I just wanted to say . . . I'm sorry if I was inappropriate in any way. I drank a lot and . . ." Pausing, he pursed his lips. "No, that's not an excuse. I'm just really sorry, is all."

Discomfort made me glance around the decadent lobby, made me tuck my hair behind my ears so many times they began to hurt. "You were fine; it's fine. Maybe you were a little flirty, but that's all. It's fine. We're fine. Nothing to talk about."

He raised his eyebrows after hearing me say *fine* almost a half dozen times, and then he shook his head. "That cab ride . . . that's something I'm not comfortable telling Kylie about, so clearly it's not fine." He slowly looked around the room, his eyes growing wearier by the second. "I guess I just can't be drunk around you."

His comment surprised me. And inflamed me with curiosity. "Why do you say that?"

He turned to look at me, and his gaze bored all the way through my soul. "Because all my walls come down around you, Valerie," he whispered. "And I'm with Kylie, so that's . . ." He let that trail off with a sigh.

The intensity of his gaze, the sadness in his voice—it cracked my chest wide open. "Yeah, I know . . ."

He suddenly looked lost as he shook his head. "You might not understand this, but . . . I'm happy being with her, Valerie. She's sweet, warm, compassionate. She laughs at my jokes and doesn't bat an eye at the crazy shifts my job requires. Things were . . . intense between you and me that night, but I'm trying not to think about that, because I really do want to be with Kylie."

Ice filled my chest. Then it turned to acid. He wanted to be with *her* . . . not me. I knew it, but hearing him say it . . . burned. Tears sprang to my eyes, but I blinked them back. "I know you do. And I want you to be with Kylie. She loves you."

Jake inhaled a deep breath, and it was almost like he was building his strength back up with the oxygen. "So we're still friends, right?"

"Of course," I said, my eyes glistening.

"Hey . . . what's going on? Everything okay?"

Blinking rapidly, I looked over to see Kylie coming out of a hallway to our right. Her eyes were narrowed as she glanced between Jake and me. *Oh God, please don't let me cry right now.* I'd never be able to explain it to her. *I* would give us away.

Throwing on a smile, I shook my head. "Nothing. Just . . . waiting for you. So what are you going to have? The steak?"

A small tear leaked from my eye, but I swiped it away so quickly there was no way she could have noticed. Right? Her inquisitive expression wasn't changing, though. Looping her arm around Jake, she said, "I don't know. But I'm definitely getting a drink." Turning to Jake, she asked, "What about you?"

Eyes glued on me, Jake shook his head. "No . . . just water for me."

His answer, his face, his apologetic eyes . . . they broke my heart right in two.

Chapter Five

Now that school was over, it was time to start weighing my options regarding work. I wanted to start making money in my chosen field, but I also didn't want to just take any job. I needed it to be an important stepping-stone, one that would help me in my goal of one day owning a restaurant. I was probably being entirely too picky, because a solid month had gone by, and I still hadn't found anything worth applying for.

"What about this one? 'Trendy, up-and-coming restaurant looking to expand their kitchen staff.' Sounds perfect."

Pausing in updating Mom's books, I looked over to see what she had found. "Hmmm, I heard about that one. Rumor has it they'll be closing their doors soon. I need something with the possibility of longevity."

Mom sighed as she shut her laptop. "You can't do our books forever, Valerie. I know that, your dad knows that, and you know it too. Eventually, you're going to need to apply for something—for *anything*. You need to get your foot in the door."

I bit my lip to stop myself from saying something petulant. She had a point, and I knew she had a point, but still . . . it was hard to settle for something I didn't really want. That was probably why I hadn't gone on any dates since meeting Jake. Everything and everyone felt like a runner-up compared to him.

Finished with Mom's books, I told her, "I should go. I'm meeting up with the girls later."

Mom raised an eyebrow at me. "Is your sister going with you?"

"I don't think so," I said, trying to sound carefree. I hadn't exactly been avoiding Kylie, but I didn't go out of my way to include her in things either. It was just . . . awkward. I hated that it was. I missed my sister. "I'm sure she's hanging out with Jake tonight anyway. They've been pretty attached at the hip lately."

Mom chuckled. "That's true. He's gone for long stretches with his job, but whenever he's home . . ." She paused to shake her head in amusement. "Kylie let it slip that she's been thinking marriage. Jake just might be *the one*."

An icy feeling struck me in the gut. It was so powerful, more like a physical blow than an emotional one, and my body reflexively curled to absorb the hit.

"You okay?" Mom asked, looking at me strangely.

Unfolding my body, I forced a smile to my face. "Of course. That's great news about Kylie. Jake seems like a good guy. I hope he asks her." Jesus, what would I do if Jake became my brother-in-law? What if he was always on the edge of my social circle, tormenting me from a distance that was entirely too close? What if I never moved on from him?

The entire drive home I wondered and worried. And then I began to think that maybe the reason I hadn't applied for a job in LA was because I didn't really want to be in LA anymore. I didn't want to watch the epic love story unfolding. And I didn't have to stay. There were exquisite culinary experiences all over the world. But then again, the thought of leaving home, of not seeing my family whenever I wanted to see them . . . it seemed a little drastic of a move. I just needed to deal with this like an adult. And the first step was applying for a job.

The minute I returned home, I turned on my computer. Might as well start applying for a position at that restaurant Mom had mentioned. Just as my computer finished booting up, there was a knock on my apartment door. Frowning at the clock, I wondered who was here. I wasn't meeting the girls for a couple of hours, and we weren't meeting here.

I opened the door, then stared in shock as Jake's jade eyes looked back at me. "What are you doing here?" I whispered. Had I fallen asleep in the car while driving home, and I was dreaming?

Jake gave me a sheepish smile. "Can I come in?"

Not sure if I wanted him inside my place, I nodded and held the door open wider. "Of course."

He walked in, and I shut the door behind him. "So what's up?"

Jake shifted on his feet. "I feel weird being here. Is this weird?"

"A little bit," I answered honestly. "Especially since I don't know why you're here."

"Oh, that . . . right."

He inhaled a deep breath, and my stomach started tingling with nerves. Why was he here? To finish what he'd almost started in the cab? Because that couldn't happen. Ever.

"The guy I've been working for is looking for a new chef's assistant. I told him all about you, and he said the job is yours if you want it."

"You . . . got me a job?" Jake telling me that he and Kylie had broken up was the only thing that would have surprised me more.

Jake cringed as he took in my expression. "Yeah. Your mom mentioned that you hadn't found anything yet, and Mr. Thomas is an amazing employer. It's a part-time job, but he pays you like it's full time. It's on his yacht, and you only work when he takes the boat out, which isn't too bad, maybe two weeks at a time, with a couple of months between trips. And you're free to get another job in between trips; you just have to be ready to go at a moment's notice."

My knees felt like they were going to give out and make me crash to the ground. "So . . . I'd be personally assisting the chef, on a yacht, for a couple of weeks every couple months . . . with you."

"Yeah," he said, shrugging.

God, it would almost be like being alone with him. We wouldn't be alone, but somehow, it still felt that way. "Why did you think of me for this?" I asked, mystified.

"Because you want to be a chef, and it's an amazing opportunity. Chef Sinclair is world renowned. He's a genius with food, and his meals are amazing. I honestly can't think of anyone better for you to work with right now. He's tough, but he'll definitely get you ready to run your own restaurant."

My mouth dropped open as excitement tingled in my belly. All of that sounded amazing—exactly what I'd been waiting for. "Wow . . . that's . . . thank you for telling me."

He gave me a small smile. "Does that mean you'll think about it?"

I nodded, and he smiled wider. "Good. Well, I guess I should get going." He looked like he was about to say something more, but then he stopped and chewed on his lip. Instead of whatever he'd been about to say, he only said, "Bye, Valerie."

He let himself out, and I couldn't stop staring at the door as he closed it behind him. What had just happened? All this time I'd been searching for the perfect job, only to be disappointed by my lack of good options. My friends had tried to help, my family had tried to help, but it was Jake who'd nailed it. Only . . . saying yes and taking this job meant being alone with him. A lot. And that was a prolonged temptation I didn't really want to endure.

I was still stewing over the strange turn of events a few hours later, when it was time to meet up with the girls. Alicia had a craving for wings, so we were meeting at the sports bar where we'd run into Jake that fateful night. When I stepped into the place, I was immediately assaulted by memories of that evening. The alcohol, the cuddling, Jake's tender touch . . . that halted kiss. Inhaling a deep breath, I banished the memories from my mind. That was not ever going to happen again.

I spotted the girls at a nearby table and raised my hand in greeting. My fingers paused halfway in the air when I realized there was an extra girl at the table. Stephanie, Alicia, Chloe, and . . . my sister. Resuming my wave, I tried to calm my surging heartbeat. I could hang out with my sister. This wasn't a big deal.

"Hey . . . everybody." Sitting down, I smiled at Kylie. "I didn't know you were going to be here. I figured you'd be with Jake."

Kylie smiled, but there was a tightness behind her eyes. "Yeah, *Chloe* invited me." Shit. Was she angry that I hadn't invited her? Her smile slipped; then she frowned. "Okay, I'm just going to say it. I haven't seen you in forever, Val. It's almost like you're avoiding me. Are you mad at me or something?"

Guilt swept through me, rampaging across my heart like a storm. "No . . . no, of course I'm not mad at you. It's just . . . I've been stressed, trying to figure out what to do after school. Nothing seems right."

Alicia snorted. "I think you should just take that job at that place I told you about."

I gave her a droll expression. "That was a grocery store."

She put a hand over her heart. "They have the best deli in the world. The cashew-chicken salad is to *die* for."

"I'll consider it," I told her with a laugh.

The waitress arrived, and the girls began giving her their orders. As Stephanie and Alicia got into a lively discussion about the waitress's boots, Kylie leaned over to me. "Jake told me he talked to you about the job offer on his employer's yacht. I think you should take it."

My eyes widened, and I twisted to face her. "Really? Do you think so?" Would she truly be okay with me working with Jake for so long, mostly alone on a boat in the middle of nowhere?

She gave me a bright, carefree smile. "Of course. It's one of those opportunities you just can't say no to. You would kick yourself forever. And Jake said the chef is some sort of amazing food guru. You would learn so much . . . it would be a mistake to say no."

Longing made me sigh. "Yeah . . . it sounds . . . pretty damn amazing." But it didn't change the fact that Jake and I would be spending a lot of time together. "Would you really be okay with that?" I asked, deciding to be forthright. "With Jake and I working together . . . like that?" I didn't want to spell it out too much for her, but she had to see that there would be a lot of potential for alone time. I wanted her to truly be okay with what she was agreeing to.

Kylie tilted her head, like she didn't understand. "Of course I'm okay with it. Is there a reason why I wouldn't be?"

Cringing that I'd given her any doubt about me at all, I shook my head. "No, of course not. I just wanted to make sure . . ." I shrugged. "It seemed like the right thing to do."

Kylie giggled, like she thought my question was cute. Alicia laughed loudly just then, distracting us from our private conversation. Kylie turned her way, so I followed suit.

"And what would you two like?" the waitress asked. "Besides my boots. Because apparently those have already been claimed."

The other girls laughed at the waitress's comment, so I laughed too. "Great, I'll have the wings, I guess."

"And to drink? There's a special on Fireball."

My stomach roiled at the mention. "No, no . . . just a beer. Something pale."

The waitress moved on to my sister, who ordered the same thing. The minute the waitress left, Alicia rounded on me. "Oh my God . . . Fireball. I'd forgotten all about that night. You and Jake were so drunk!"

Embarrassment and guilt raced up my spine. *Could we please talk about something else? Anything else.* "We weren't that drunk," I said, trying to make it seem like Alicia was exaggerating. From the corner of my eye, I could see Kylie intently watching me. *Please don't mention we were cuddly. Please don't mention that we shared a cab at the end of the night.*

In response to my comment, Alicia tossed her hands into the air. "More shots!" she screeched, mimicking me.

I wanted to crawl into a deep dark hole, but thankfully, Steph skillfully changed the subject. "Be nice, Alicia. She was just celebrating a once-in-a-lifetime moment, and we've all overindulged in times like that. Like when you caught your boyfriend cheating on you and we all helped you drown your sorrows?"

Alicia grabbed her head, like she instantly had a headache. "God, don't remind me. About him or the drinking."

The topic of conversation thankfully moved away from me then, onto the other girls and their over-the-top nights. I relaxed as we joked around about other subjects. My sister relaxed, too, letting whatever odd thoughts she might have had die.

The entire time we ate, drank, and laughed, I thought about Kylie's comments about this yacht job. She'd made it sound so appealing, a once-in-a-lifetime chance, but it meant being enclosed on a ship with the man of my dreams. Who was also the man of *her* dreams. I wanted the opportunity, but I didn't want to torture myself. I honestly had no idea what to do.

Exhaustion took me over when I finally got back home, and I collapsed on my bed in a heap. This really shouldn't have been such a monumental decision. It was a chance to work with a renowned chef one-on-one. If I took Jake completely out of the equation, my decision was easy. Take the job! In addition to paying well, it would be an adventure and a great learning experience. The answer seemed so simple, so why was my mind spinning?

Jake. His smile, his eyes, his shaggy hair, his sensuous lips. He was undeniably alluring, and he'd be all too tempting on the open ocean. But the job . . . that was an even bigger temptation.

I dug through my bag and found my cell phone. Jake's number was already programmed. Sometime during that fateful drunken night, we'd exchanged numbers. Biting my lip, I debated if I should give my answer to him or my sister. He was the connection to the job, though, so I decided to send my message to him.

Tell your boss I want the job.

A long exhale left me after I hit send. Then my nerves spiked as doubt crept inside. Jake's response was just a moment behind my text. Good. I'll tell him tomorrow. The job starts next Tuesday.

My heart was pounding in my chest as I read his words. We hadn't had many reasons to directly talk to each other since our drunken evening. It made me a little heady to know he was thinking about me right now.

Thank you, I texted back. I couldn't help but wonder if he was with Kylie right now. She hadn't mentioned meeting up with him after dinner, but she certainly could have. I didn't want to ask him, but curiosity was killing me. Kylie mentioned how great the chef is. She pushed me to say yes.

You saw her tonight? he responded.

Yeah. She came to dinner with the girls. She didn't come over after? God, that wasn't super obvious, was it?

His response took a little bit longer. No, I'm alone.

I had to close my eyes, because that almost sounded like an invitation. A part of me wanted to tell him I was alone too. A part of me wanted to invite myself over. A part of me wanted to tell him I adored him. But all I told him was, Good night, Jake. See you Tuesday.

Chapter Six

I was a nervous wreck waiting for Tuesday to arrive, so nervous that I actually got sick a couple of times. But when it finally arrived, when it was finally time for me to head out on this journey, I was more excited than anything else. This was it! My dream was coming true. Or at least one more step in the dream.

The nerves returned, however, when I stepped onto the deck of the most luxurious yacht I'd ever seen. It was absolutely breathtaking, and I had to pinch myself to confirm that this was real, that this floating piece of art was where I'd be working for the next two weeks. Stunned, I just kept looking around at all the finery. I had to force myself to close my mouth and act professional; I wanted to make a good impression on my new employer and my new mentor. Straightening my shoulders, I lifted my chin and settled my rampaging emotions. I could do this. No problem.

Looking around the gleaming, polished beauty, I wondered where I should go first. The instructions I'd received from my *welcome aboard* email hadn't been entirely clear. I supposed I could just wander around, looking for the crew's quarters, or I could try and find my boss so I could check in with him, or I could seek out my new office—the kitchen. Or galley, I guessed, since we were on a boat.

A smile stretched across my lips as joy bubbled to the surface. I couldn't wait to get down to the galley and start cooking. I'd wanted something meaningful for my first job after culinary school, and it didn't get much more unique than being a personal chef on a billionaire's private yacht.

As it turned out, my new employer, Jonathon Thomas, was some Silicon Valley tech genius who'd made a fortune early in life and now spent an enormous amount of his free time on the water. As I'd discovered upon filling out the paperwork and being officially hired, this really was an amazing job. Mr. Thomas paid his employees ridiculously well. We just had to be ready to go to work whenever he needed us. So essentially, his entire staff was on call 24-7, 365. That would take some getting used to, but Jake swore it was worth it.

Figuring that everything I needed was below me, I made my way to the stairs. A familiar face was coming up them when I got there. Jake. He was humming a song as he walked up the stairs, and my heart squeezed when I deciphered the tune—it was one of my all-time favorites. We had so much in common; it was so unfair that it didn't matter.

A small smile spread over Jake's face when he noticed me. It made a swarm of butterflies tickle my stomach, and I hated that it did. How were we going to do this? "Valerie," he said, stepping up to me. "You made it." His green eyes sparkled in the sunlight as his smile widened, and I had to suppress a sigh. It was already difficult, and we'd only just begun.

"Yeah . . . thank you for the directions. I definitely would have gotten lost without them."

Jake nodded. Then his gaze fell to our feet. "You ready for this?" he asked, peeking up at me.

The question seemed full of double meaning. *Are you ready for your new job, and are you ready to be locked on a ship with me for two weeks?* In truth, I wasn't ready for either of those things. "Yeah, sure . . . one hundred percent."

Jake's eyes narrowed as he studied me, but he didn't question my bravado. Instead he said, "You don't get seasick, do you? I probably should have asked you that before I mentioned the job."

I felt my cheeks flush as his question struck a nerve. Did he somehow know I had a weak stomach? "No, no, I'm fine on the water." That was almost true. So long as I was doped up on Dramamine, I was great.

"Good," he said, smiling awkwardly.

We stood there, staring at each other for a few more uncomfortable seconds, before I motioned down the stairs. "Do you think you could show me where to go? This boat is so much bigger than I thought it was going to be."

Jake let out a nervous laugh. "Yeah, right. Sorry. I know what you mean. It took me five months to figure out where everything was. Of course, I spend most of my time on the bridge, so I suppose that's to be expected." Jake was just assisting the captain right now, but someday, he'd be piloting this massive barge. And somehow, that made him even hotter.

Running a hand through his hair, Jake indicated the stairs with his head. "This way." He started walking down them, and I took the opportunity of his absent gaze to appreciate his backside. His body was incredible, from what I could tell, at least. The most I'd ever seen of him was his bare legs in shorts and his bare arms peeking out from a T-shirt that was tight against his chest, flat against his abs. My sister had invited me to the beach with them once before, but I'd said no. Seeing him shirtless . . . God, I didn't think I could take it. Especially not in front of Kylie. I'd be visibly shaken, and she'd instantly know for sure that I craved her boyfriend.

With a sigh, I followed Jake down the stairs to my new home away from home. Rooms for the crew were on the very bottom level of the ship, which seemed fitting, I supposed, since it wasn't our boat and we weren't on vacation. There were eight of us working this trip. Jake, another guy, and the captain on the bridge; the chef and me in the kitchen; Mr. Thomas's personal assistant, who was almost always by his side, from what Jake said; and the two women who kept the yacht looking picture perfect at all times—Mr. Thomas's request. He was a bit of a neat freak from what Jake had told me, something that might be an issue for me, since I could be a bit of a slob. I didn't want him to fire me because my station was too messy. Not that he probably ventured into the kitchen much. Or at all. I probably wouldn't even see him this trip.

"All right, here we go. This room is yours." Jake opened a slim door with a flourish, showing me an equally slim room. There was only enough space inside for a one-person bed and a thin dresser. While I wondered if I'd feel claustrophobic sleeping in a room no larger than my bathroom back home, Jake pointed down the hallway. "Mine is at the other end . . ." He worked his lip after he said that, and confusion, desire, and guilt flooded through me. He was going to be so close to me, yet so far.

Not wanting to dwell on the sparks between us, sparks we were both choosing to ignore, I raised my hand. Jake laughed at the gesture, and some of the tension dissolved. "Yes?" he said.

"Bathroom?" I asked, setting my bag on my bed.

After seeing the size of the rooms, I knew what Jake was going to say, but I was still disappointed when he said it. "We all share one bathroom. It's over here."

While I groaned internally, Jake showed me the one tiny bathroom we'd all be sharing. It was only big enough for a toilet, a sink, and a small stand-up shower. Guess all the fineries were upstairs. Oh well. It was only for a couple of weeks.

"Yeah, I know," he said. "It's not the greatest, but the rest of the job is, I swear." While I absently nodded, Jake added, "There's only one rule with the bathroom, though. If you're showering, you have to leave the door unlocked so people can still pee."

My eyes sprang wide open in alarm, and I snapped my head to the left to stare at him in shock. "What?" The shower curtain was clear plastic—completely see through. I could *not* imagine Jake walking in on me naked. Or vice versa. My heart started thudding as I contemplated that.

Jake cringed, then sighed. "Sorry, bad joke. Just trying to make this less . . . strange."

I exhaled in relief, then nodded. "I don't want this to be weird, Jake. You and I . . . we're friends, remember? And friends can . . . hang out without it being weird."

He stared at me for a long time, then finally nodded. Then he smiled, a full, glorious smile; it was like the sun coming out on a cloudy day. "Come on, I'll show you the galley. You're gonna love it."

His grin filled me with warmth, and I knew that even if I somehow hated the galley, I was going to love him showing it to me. Jake led me to the stairs, then up one level. After a long hallway, we finally reached the galley. My mood soared when I saw it. Where the bedrooms were small and disappointing, the galley was glorious. I'd been expecting it to be on the tiny side, but it was much bigger than I'd imagined, and everything was top notch. We hadn't had anything nearly this nice at school, and we'd had some nice equipment. My mind started racing with possibilities, and my imagination exploded as I opened the fridge and saw exotic ingredient after exotic ingredient. The sky was the limit in this kitchen. I could make . . . anything.

"Oh my God, Jake . . . this is incredible." I looked over to see him watching me with a small smile on his face, hands stuffed casually in the pockets of his loose khakis. "Thank you so much for getting me this job. I can't tell you how much it means to me." *How much you mean to me.*

His smile grew into a charming grin that made my heart flutter. "I had a feeling you'd appreciate this, and I knew you'd be perfect for the position. This is where you're supposed to be, Valerie." The softness of his voice, the look of admiration and respect on his face—they made an ache surge through my chest, tightening painfully around my heart. He was just so . . .

Ugh. If only I'd met him first. If only this feeling that cropped up whenever he was around didn't have to be smashed into a million pieces. If only he were mine.

Stop. This was going to be a really long trip—and an absolute nightmare of a job—if I kept letting myself dwell on those kinds of thoughts. He made my sister incredibly happy, and I absolutely adored the fact that she was so content. She deserved to be. She'd been waiting for a man like Jake for a long time. I needed to shift my focus and keep it shifted. Luckily for me, the chef stepped into the room, and he proved to be quite the distraction.

He was a big barrel-chested man with shocking red hair and commanding eyes. He barely gave Jake a glance before locking his eyes on me. "You must be my new assistant. I hope you're ready for this. The last assistant I had left the boat in tears halfway through the trip."

My eyes widened in surprise. I hadn't known about any drama with the previous assistant. I shifted my gaze to Jake. He had a sheepish look on his face, like he was suddenly feeling very sorry for withholding vital information about the job. Well, I could handle diva bosses. It couldn't be that much different than my instructors at school, and I'd survived that just fine.

"Ready and willing," I told Chef, clasping my hands behind my back. He looked impressed, and I noticed Jake smiling at me in my peripheral. Chef turned to Jake, like he'd noticed him too. "You can go, pool boy. Thank you for showing her the way."

Jake frowned at him. "How many times do I have to tell you to stop calling me that, Luis?"

Chef raised a red eyebrow. "Probably about as many times as I have to ask you to stop calling me Luis. My name is Chef Sinclair." He made a shooing motion with his hand. "Now get out of my galley. We have work to do."

Jake sighed, then looked over at me. "Good luck. I'll check in with you later tonight." From the look on his face, I knew I was going to earn every penny of my paycheck this trip. That was fine. I wasn't afraid of hard work.

"Thank you so much, Jake."

He nodded, then hurriedly scooted out the door.

I inhaled a deep breath, steeling my nerves, then twisted to my new supervisor. "What do we need to do first?" I asked.

"Everything," he answered, tossing a chef's jacket at me.

His answer made a surge of trepidation wash through me, but it was quickly replaced by glee as I stared at the jacket in my hands. A real, honest-to-God chef's jacket. True, this one was a uniform provided for me by someone else, but the symbolism was the same. I'd done it. I was living my dream.

After putting it on, I quickly snapped a selfie and texted it to Stephanie. I made it, Steph! I'm a real chef!

Her reply was instant. OMG! You're so cute! Before I could slip my phone back in my pocket, she texted me again. Have a great trip! And don't worry about being stuck on a boat with Jake. You're a strong woman, you'll be fine. She ended that statement with a huge smiling face, but it still made a wash of nervous energy flow through me. Fine. Right.

I was just about to put my phone away when a loud bang sounded throughout the galley. Panic made me jump, and my heart instantly started racing. I glanced around for the source of the noise, wondering what had just exploded. What I saw was Chef Sinclair, hands clasped around a huge butcher's block that he'd just smacked on the counter. "No cell phones in my galley. Ever. Put it away."

Trying to get my surging heart to calm down, I nodded and put the phone back in my pocket. Then I quickly took it out and turned the sound off, just in case. "Sorry, Chef. Won't happen again."

"I know," he said, expression devoid of humor. "Now, let's start prepping lunch; then we'll work on dinner."

Several hours later, I finally had a chance to stop and breathe. Working with Chef Sinclair was intense, to say the least, but I'd already learned so much more than I'd thought I would. He might be cold and rude, but Chef knew his stuff, so I paid attention to every word he said. Like Jake had said, this man could be the key to me running a successful restaurant one day.

My only problem with the job so far was the lack of windows in the galley. It took me a few hours into the shift to finally notice that the yacht was no longer resting peacefully at the dock. The thought of being in an enclosed space surrounded by nothing but miles of water made my heart grow icy with worry, but at least we were floating on top of the water, not submerged beneath it like a submarine. I didn't think I could ever be deep under the water like that. I'd hyperventilate so badly I'd have to be sedated. I'd take floating on top any day, although that came with its own problems.

Once I realized the ship was moving, I became all too aware of the incessant swaying motion. Chef Sinclair moved around the galley with a relaxed, comfortable stance, like it was completely natural to have the floor constantly alternate its slight tilt. I wasn't so coordinated and spent a lot of time taking little extra steps to correct my balance, like I was tap-dancing. It was ridiculous. And embarrassing. It made me happy that Jake was up top, on the bridge, so he didn't have to witness my absolute lack of grace. At least the Dramamine was doing its job, and I wasn't queasy.

Chef Sinclair plopped a plate of the dinner we'd made on the small table in front of me. "Here, eat up. Then you're free for the night."

I stared at the steaming plate like it held my salvation. Thank God. I was starving and exhausted, and every inch of me was sore. All I wanted to do was eat and then lie down in my tiny room. Or maybe check out the upper deck. I had to imagine it was beautiful up there at night, with stars everywhere you looked.

"Thank you," I politely told the chef.

He nodded, making a gruff noise in his throat. "You did all right today. You didn't mess up too many things, and you didn't cry. That's pretty good in my book. I'm going to head to my room; tomorrow comes early." I could see the exhaustion in his face, and it made me feel a little better to know I wasn't the only one who was tired. "Make sure you keep your jacket on if you go upstairs. Mr. Thomas likes to see everyone in uniform at all times."

He rolled his eyes like he thought that was ridiculous, and then he turned and left me to eat my meal in peace. And my God, it was the best meal I'd ever had in all my life. This trip was going to ruin me on good food, I could tell.

When I was finished with my meal, I washed my plate and silverware, dried them, and then put them away. Jake had warned me that Mr. Thomas was a neat freak, and I had a feeling Chef Sinclair was too. With that in mind, I wiped off the table and the counters, just in case. Once everything was as sparkling as I'd found it, I left the galley and headed out to explore the rest of the ship. The parts I could see, anyway. I didn't want to bother Jake on the bridge, and I wasn't sure if I could go up there anyway, and Mr. Thomas's personal cabins were definitely off limits. Mainly, I wandered the hallways, peeking into rooms that were dripping with wealth. It made me a little uneasy to touch anything, and I longed for my simple, tiny bedroom. But first . . . outside.

Joyfully, I climbed the steps that would lead me to the upper deck. The fact that I made it all the way up there without running into anyone spoke volumes about the size of the ship. What one man needed a boat this size for was a mystery to me.

Out on the deck, the cool breeze stroked my face, teased the small, loose strands of hair resting along my cheeks. I pulled my hair out of the tight bun I'd had it corralled in all day long and let the wind blow my blonde locks about in a frenzy of movement. Grinning at the freedom, I stepped to the railing and peeked out over the dark rippling water around me. The moon was full and bright, casting silver light over the water, highlighting each undulating peak. Billions of twinkling stars dotted the sky, and as my gaze shifted up, I tried to pick out the familiar patterns that formed the constellations.

"Incredible, isn't it?"

I glanced behind me to see Jake walking my way, and my heart stuttered in my chest. Dear God . . . he was wearing a military-inspired uniform that made him look like a member of the navy. I didn't think I'd ever seen him more attractive than he was right now. Once my heart settled, my pulse quickened. He shouldn't be out here with me, especially when he looked like that.

"The view? Yeah, it's pretty amazing," I said, trying to sound casual and unaffected by him.

A small smile on his lips, he joined me at the railing. As he looked out over the water, I studied his face. The jade green was bluer in the silver light. His lips fuller, like the moon wanted me to kiss him. This was so stupid. Just staring at him had my heart racing. This was where I should have excused myself, but somehow, I couldn't. I inched closer to him instead.

My movement jarred him from whatever thoughts had distracted him. He just stared at me for a quiet moment, and I was thankful he couldn't see my pulse thundering through my veins. Three weeks. That was the time difference between him meeting my sister and him meeting me. I still relived that first encounter in my mind sometimes; I thought I'd fallen for him right then and there. Life had a cruel sense of humor sometimes.

"So how was your first day?" he asked, his smile warm as he leaned against the yacht's railing.

I sighed as I remembered all the aches I was going to feel tomorrow. "Tiring. But amazing. Thank you, again." He opened his mouth to object, but I beat him to it. "I know I've said that about a million times already, but honestly, Jake, with all the . . . awkwardness between us, you could have kept your mouth shut and let the opportunity pass me by, but you didn't, so I'm going to keep saying thank you."

He frowned. "I wouldn't say things have been . . . awkward."

I raised an eyebrow at that, and Jake sighed as he looked over at the calm water. "Okay, maybe it's been a little awkward. I just feel so damn . . . guilty around you."

"Why?" I asked, inadvertently stepping closer to him.

"You know why," he said, looking down at me with a haunted expression. "That night . . . in the cab. I still think about it, even though I know I shouldn't. I just . . ."

His eyes flicked over my face as his words trailed off. Then his gaze settled on my lips, and I knew exactly what was on his mind. I inhaled a deep breath, then held it so long my lungs felt like they were about to burst. We shouldn't be talking about this, shouldn't be reminiscing about it like it was a fond memory. We'd gone too far that night. We couldn't do it again.

With only the sound of the waves licking the sides of the ship, Jake's hand lifted. His fingertips touched my face, and his expression shifted into one of deep longing. "Valerie . . . I think . . ."

Seeing his turmoil, feeling it myself, I pulled away from him. "I think I should go and . . . get some rest. As Chef Sinclair says, tomorrow comes early."

Jake was still leaning against the railing, still watching me with longing in his eyes. "Yeah . . . all right. Good night, Valerie," he whispered.

My heart felt cracked wide open as I walked away from him, and all I really wanted to do was turn around and throw myself into his arms. I loved my sister, but it was so hard to not want him. This was going to be a very long trip. Maybe this was a bad idea after all.

Chapter Seven

I tossed and turned all night long for the next several evenings. The job was stressful and intense, but that was only making me exhausted. It was Jake who was making me restless. He was constantly checking up on me, making sure I was okay, constantly staring at me with confusion in his eyes. It was excruciating being around him, and yet I longed for it, too . . . longed for him. When I got back home, I might look into seeing a therapist. Obsessing about someone I couldn't have had to be unhealthy.

I couldn't stop doing it, though. I'd known it was going to be hard being around him so much, but I hadn't imagined it would be *this* hard. Maybe if he weren't attracted to me, too, it would be easier. If he were just nice, supportive, comforting, without being so . . . pained, then maybe I could stop fantasizing about him.

Sticking to my new routine, I groggily stepped out of bed and immediately banged my knee against the dresser. I was loving my new job, but I was also looking forward to returning to my larger bedroom; it was gargantuan compared to this place.

I grabbed my work clothes and toiletries, then opened my door to head to the communal bathroom. That was another thing I was looking forward to having again—a private bathroom. Jake's door opened at the same time as mine. He smiled when he saw me, then slowly started walking my way. From the shampoo and towel in his hand, I could tell he wanted to use the bathroom too.

He let out a nervous laugh when we stopped in front of the same door. "And here's the problem when people start their shift around the same time and there's only one bathroom."

I cringed, then indicated the door. "It's fine; you go first. I'm sure you'll be much quicker about it than me."

He smiled at me, and I had to stop myself from sighing. "Are you sure? I don't mind waiting."

I forced a carefree smile to my face. "Yeah, I'm sure. Go ahead. I'll just . . . wait here."

Jake nodded, then quickly opened the door. Pausing in the frame, he said, "I'll just be a sec."

The door closed, and I let my head fall back against the wall behind me. God. Now he was in there stripping off all his clothes, and I had to stand here picturing him in all his glory. Maybe it was time for me to admit defeat and go home. But this job . . . I desperately didn't want to give it up. It was everything I'd been looking for and more. Working with Chef Sinclair was a blessing. It was exactly the sort of experience I'd been hoping for. I had no choice but to tough this out.

Even though Jake took the fastest shower known to man, it felt like he was in there forever. Of course, it didn't help that I kept inadvertently picturing soap bubbles trailing across his skin. But eventually the door cracked open, and I pushed off against the wall, relieved that the torture was over. Only it wasn't. When Jake stepped out of the bathroom, he was only wearing a towel wrapped around his waist.

My eyes widened as I stared at him. I'd avoided seeing him half-dressed just for this very reason. I didn't want this cruel vision of perfection burned into my brain, and it definitely was now. The towel was low on his waist, showcasing his abs like in some sort of erotic game show. And my God, his stomach . . . up until this exact second, I hadn't believed that real men had muscles that defined. It was as if every line had been chiseled into him by a master sculptor. His chest, his arms . . . every part of him begged for contact. How had my sister never once mentioned how cut he was?

Jake smiled softly as he indicated the steaming bathroom he'd just vacated. "All yours."

I quickly snapped my mouth shut. And that was when I noticed it. Jesus. He had a freaking tattoo. Kylie had never mentioned that either. There were two lines of script traveling down his side. I ached to read what it said, but his arm was partially in the way, and I was too riled up to carry on a coherent conversation. Instead, I muttered, "Thanks," and darted into the bathroom, quick as lightning.

I showered with cold water, hoping that would snap that glorious body out of my head. No such luck. It was stuck there, much as I was stuck on this boat with him. But I was learning a lot, and that was what mattered—the job.

After dressing in the tiny bathroom, I hastily stashed my stuff in my room and headed to the galley. I held my breath the entire time I was downstairs, wondering if and when Jake would appear again. I wasn't quite ready to see him after that last encounter. I would have to ask him not to do that anymore . . . and that would open the door to yet another awkward conversation.

When I got to the galley, Chef Sinclair was already there, along with a tall, distinguished-looking man whom I'd never seen before. Chef Sinclair looked nervous having him in his kitchen, and that was when it struck me—this was our mutual boss, the head honcho, the billionaire, Mr. Thomas. Why was he down here and not upstairs in his luxurious palace, lounging on furniture that cost more than everything in my apartment combined? Shit. Was I about to get fired? Would that be a bad thing?

Yes, I wanted this job.

Chef Sinclair locked eyes with me when he spotted me entering. He subtly adjusted his jacket, and I did the same. Mr. Thomas was a neat freak who wanted all of his employees in crisp, clean uniforms. I hoped mine wasn't wrinkled.

Mr. Thomas turned around and met eyes with me. He had a friendly face but penetrating eyes. It was almost like he could see into the very depths of my soul. "Ah," he said. "You must be the new assistant. Chef Sinclair tells me that you're doing well and that he put last night's main course largely in your hands."

I felt like I was going to be sick. Had I messed up the beef Wellington? Had he gotten sick? Chef Sinclair had said the last assistant had asked to leave midtrip. How did that work? As far as I knew, we were in the middle of nowhere, somewhere in the South Pacific. Would they just put me in a life raft with instructions to paddle in an easterly direction? I hoped not. I wasn't the greatest paddler. And sharks terrified me.

"Yes. I . . . hope you liked it." Mentally, I crossed my fingers and prayed for good news.

Mr. Thomas stared at me for long, achingly quiet moments, and then he smiled. "I loved it, and I wanted to congratulate you personally on a meal well done."

Relief surged through me so fast I thought my knees might buckle. My grin was too big to be professional, but I didn't care. He'd loved it. Even though I felt like jumping up and down, I kept my comment brief and restrained. "Thank you, sir."

"You're very welcome. Good job—keep it up." Turning to Chef Sinclair, he added, "Captain tells me we might hit the edge of a storm today. Make sure everything is strapped down tight. I don't want any accidents."

Chef Sinclair nodded. "Will do, sir."

Mr. Thomas nodded, then left the galley. The second he was gone, I started bouncing up and down. "Oh my God! Oh my God, Chef! He loved it!"

Chef watched my exuberant display with pursed lips. "I heard."

Forgetting all my decorum, I ran up to him and gave him a quick hug. "Thank you so much for all you've taught me. This has truly been a dream come true."

Chef Sinclair rigidly pushed me away. "Clearly, I haven't taught you professionalism yet, but . . . you're welcome." His expression softened into a smile. "You know, I don't say this to my assistants often, but . . . I truly believe you have potential, and if you stick with this—and don't give up when it gets hard, because it *will* get hard—then I think you could actually have a very successful restaurant one day."

My jaw nearly dropped to the floor after such kind words from him. "Thank you," I murmured. "Someone like you saying that . . . it means more than you know."

He smirked in response. "You forget I was once in your position. I know *exactly* what it means. Now don't let it go to your head." Shooing me off, he said, "Let's get ready for breakfast. And keep in mind what Mr. Thomas said. Everything gets put away after you use it. Everything. Every time. It might get a little bumpy, and I don't want anything breaking."

I was so happy I was giddy . . . right up until he said that, and then a hole of anxiety began opening inside my stomach. "Bumpy? How bumpy?"

Chef shrugged, like he wasn't concerned at all. "Depends on how much of the storm catches us. I wouldn't worry too much about it. Captain is a genius about avoiding these things. We'll be fine."

"Oh, okay . . . good." Because I was sure I'd need about five more Dramamine to cope with anything greater than the constant slight swaying that I was slowly becoming accustomed to.

Putting everything away after it was used was a gigantic pain in the ass. And I kept forgetting to do it. Chef Sinclair had to constantly remind me to wash that pan and put it back, to not leave food out, to keep the knives on the magnetic board. It was a hassle, and since the boat was still only slightly swaying, it felt completely unnecessary. But all that changed while we were making dinner.

I heard the rain first, which was odd, since it was loud in the kitchen and we were a couple of floors down from the top deck. I usually didn't hear anything from outside. Then the gentle rocking of the boat became more pronounced. I lost my balance a few times and had to slap a hand onto the counter to remain upright. Panic shot through me, and I looked to the chef for comfort.

"What's going on?" I asked, hoping my voice didn't sound as high strung as I felt.

"Looks like the storm caught us," he said. "But we'll be fine. This is nothing the boat can't handle." His voice was calm and comforting, but his eyes were a little too wide, his forehead a little too wrinkled. He was worried, and knowing that he was concerned didn't make me feel any better.

I was in the process of cutting up a zucchini when a sudden violent jolt shoved me against the counter. My hand slipped, and the knife slid across my finger. Bright blood seeped to the surface of my skin, followed by pain. "Damn it," I swore, grabbing a paper towel.

Chef threw a concerned look my way. "You okay?"

"Yeah, just sliced myself." I traded the paper towel for a bandage just as another jolt sent the zucchini and knife flying to the floor. If we hadn't been so diligent about putting stuff away, I was sure half the kitchen would have shifted. "This seems bad. Are we still okay?"

Chef didn't seem like he was sure anymore. He thought for a moment, then picked up a phone that connected us to the bridge. "What the hell is going on up there?" he said.

Someone on deck responded, probably Jake, but all I heard was Chef saying, "I see. Okay."

He hung up the phone, and dread filled my stomach. "What?"

"We're closing the kitchen. We ran right into the storm, and there's no getting out of it now."

Well, shit.

Heart racing, I helped Chef put away the few things we hadn't secured yet, and then we double-checked everything. When we were both satisfied that nothing was going to move in the room, we turned off the lights and left.

"What do we do now?" I asked.

"Just go to your room and stay put. Best to wait these things out somewhere safe."

Yeah . . . somewhere safe. Problem was, nothing really felt safe at the moment. The violent jerking wasn't stopping, and every other minute, I was being tossed against one wall or another. This was definitely not normal. "Are you sure we're going to be okay?" I knew Chef couldn't possibly know what our fate would be, but I still needed to ask. My mind needed reassurance, even if it was false assurance.

"Of course," he said, a tight smile on his lips. "See you bright and early tomorrow."

"Yes, Chef," I automatically replied, and somehow the normalcy of saying that to him made me feel a little better.

He turned and left, and I watched him for a moment before inhaling a deep breath and making a mad dash to the safety of my tiny room. At least I wouldn't be tossed around too badly in there—there wasn't enough space.

After shutting the door, I lay on my bed and tried to calm my rolling stomach. Either the Dramamine was wearing off, or the drug wasn't strong enough to offset the extreme rocking of the ship. I was both terrified and nauseous. But through it all, my main concern was Jake. Was he still up top, helping the captain keep control of the ship, or had he been dismissed to his room? A part of me—a large part—wanted to pop into his bedroom to check on him. Getting through this with him by my side sounded preferable to toughing it out alone.

Maybe in a minute. When my stomach wasn't threatening to spill out onto the floor.

The boat kept jerking left and right, up and down. I clamped onto the mattress, holding myself in place as best I could as I prayed for the storm to stop. And that was when I heard and felt something alarming. The entire ship groaned, the metal walls around me vibrating with noise. It was a terrifying sound, one that made my heart pound in my chest, made my palms slick with sweat. I knew nothing about boats, but I instinctively knew that sound wasn't good. It stopped with a loud metallic cracking that reverberated through my bones, and then the boat shifted in an entirely new direction. The shift was so sudden and severe that I couldn't keep myself from slamming into the headboard. As I lay at an odd angle against the wall, I waited for the boat to correct itself. It didn't.

An alarm started sounding throughout the ship, a loud, shrill siren that was straight out of my worst nightmare. The strange angle of the ship combined with that sound meant only one thing—we were in trouble, and we weren't getting out of it. Panic made me shoot off the bed. I heard people in the hallway, so I tossed open the door. Crew members were scrambling to get to the stairs. It was difficult with the way the ship was tilted. I followed them, praying that Jake and the captain could fix this, somehow. That was when I heard the captain's voice over the intercom, ordering everyone to get to the life rafts. Oh God . . . we were going under.

The group of us emerged on the floor just under the top deck. Even more people were rushing to the stairs here—including Chef Sinclair and Mr. Thomas. They all looked terrified. Not able to take the terror I saw in their eyes, I glanced out the large windows lining the ship. And that was when I saw the waterline. It was rising above the windows as we slipped at a steep angle under the roiling ocean. I stared in utter horror as the slit of sky transformed into endless ocean. My mind was stuck trying to process it. We were sinking. Why were we sinking? Boats floated. They only sank when there was . . .

A hole.

Even as I thought it, I heard the sound of rushing, angry water coming to claim me. Coming to claim us all. People were screaming as they tried to leave, but I knew in my gut they were too late. They wouldn't beat the water. None of us would. This wasn't supposed to happen. This was my dream; it was supposed to be the beginning of my life, not the end.

As I stood there, transfixed by my fate, I heard a voice shouting my name. "Valerie!"

I looked over at the stairs to see Jake pushing against people as he ran *down* them. Ran to me. Why was he running to me? He was safer near the surface. "Jake!"

I moved toward him, fingers outstretched. We were centimeters from connecting when the wall of water hit us. We were slammed forward, against the wall next to the stairs. The impact nearly made me pass out, but somehow I stayed conscious. When my world settled somewhat, I opened my eyes and looked through the murky water full of random floating objects. Up. I needed to go up and get out. That was all I truly cared about—escape. The lights in the boat flickered, then died, plunging me into complete darkness. No. If I couldn't see, how would I ever leave? I couldn't blindly search for the stairs; I didn't have enough air. This beautiful ship was about to be my watery grave.

No. It couldn't end like this.

Panic made me spin in a circle. Where were the stairs? Where were all the people who'd been on them? Where was Jake?

A second later, a hand grabbed mine, stopping my ceaseless spinning. Another hand grabbed my face, focusing me. Jake. He was so close I could see him clearly despite the darkness. He looked scared as he floated there in front of me but focused too. When he saw I was paying attention to him, he jerked his thumb behind him. He knew where the stairs were. Thank God. But did it even matter at this point? My lungs were burning, and the pressure against my ears told me we were still sinking. We could already be too deep to make it to the surface in time.

Jake's hand tightened around mine, and he yanked me toward the stairs. We kicked and pulled our way up them before leaving the ship's interior and entering the open ocean. There was enough fading daylight streaming through the water to show me a nightmarish vision—the entire crew trapped in the hostile ocean, the surface several dozens of feet above us. The suction of the boat had pulled everyone deeper than I'd imagined it would. I wasn't sure I had enough strength or enough air to make it out of the water. Some of the people had already succumbed to the ocean; they were completely still as they floated, arms and legs outstretched in an almost peaceful manner. Mr. Thomas was one of them. He'd never leave these waters that he loved so much. Some of the surviving crew members, still struggling to reach air, were bleeding badly; the impact with the water hadn't been as kind to them as it had been to me. Even if they did break the surface, I didn't think they'd live long.

Just when I was wondering how Jake and I would ever escape this hell, I felt clothes being removed from me. Jake was hurriedly tugging at my jacket. He'd already pulled off his and kicked off his shoes. He was trying to reduce our drag. I followed suit, slipping off my shoes, removing my chef's jacket. Once we were more streamlined, Jake grabbed my hand, kicked off the deck, and shot toward the surface like a torpedo, yanking me with him until I matched his fierce, kicking stride.

Out of the corner of my eye, I spotted another survivor—Chef Sinclair. He was struggling toward the surface but not moving nearly as quickly as Jake and me. His face was full of fear, and as I watched, his mouth reflexively opened, and he sucked in water. No. He was failing, drowning; he'd never make it to the surface without help.

I started to let go of Jake's hand, wanting to save my mentor. Jake clamped me tight, then glanced down at my face. Seeing my expression, he shot a brief look over at what had my attention. He studied Chef Sinclair for a microsecond, then shook his head, held me tighter, and kept on kicking toward the surface. Chef noticed us as we shot by him. His hand briefly extended toward mine, while my hand reached out for him. Our fingers touched . . . and a second later, the light of life left his eyes. Forever.

I knew, right then and there, if I happened to make it out of this alive, that blank stare would fill my every waking thought and haunt every single one of my dreams. *I'm so sorry, Chef.*

Chapter Eight

We kicked for what felt like an eternity. My vision was hazy, and my lungs were screaming at me to breathe. I wasn't going to make it. I was going to end up like Chef, gulping down seawater, filling my lungs until I sank to the bottom of the ocean with the doomed yacht.

Just when I couldn't handle another second without oxygen, we finally broke the surface of the frigid water. I gulped in much-needed air. *Thank God, we made it.* I felt like sobbing as I floated on top of the raging waves. Relief that I was alive surged through me, giving me strength, but heartache and guilt filled me too. No one else had popped above the surface yet.

As waves crashed around us, dousing us with water, I swiveled my head, looking for other survivors. I fiercely hoped someone else had made it to the surface, but everywhere I turned, all I saw was the chaotic, angry ocean, barren of all life, save us. They hadn't made it . . . none of them. Mr. Thomas and the rest of the crew were now forever trapped under the vast depths, their lungs full of water, holding them down. Jake and I were the only ones to make it out, but we were nowhere near safe yet. We couldn't tread water forever, especially with how vicious the waves were. With every movement of my arms and legs, I felt myself slipping back under the water, and I knew if I went under again, I'd never resurface.

Jake seemed just as stunned as me as he looked around. The horror of what had happened was too much to bear. My mind was still struggling to believe this was real, so I had to believe Jake was suffering from the same problem. He snapped out of it quickly, though. Looking back at me, he nodded with his head. “Over there.”

I glanced at where he’d indicated and saw a flat piece of . . . something floating on the water. It looked like part of the rear deck. Jake started swimming toward it, and I followed suit. It was difficult. I was so tired. I’d always thought I was in good shape before, but I suddenly felt like I hadn’t exercised in years. Escaping to the surface had taken nearly everything I had. Jake too. He was breathing heavily when we finally reached our salvation.

Jake used his arms to pull himself up; the slab of wood slanted sharply as he did, but he was able to move himself into position and steady the material. I didn’t have that kind of strength left, and I lifted my hand, silently asking for assistance. Jake splayed out on the board for stability, then grabbed my arm and yanked me up with him. It hurt, but I wasn’t about to complain. The ache in my shoulder would heal, assuming we lived through this.

Once I was fully on top of the deck with him, I lay on my stomach and panted. I couldn’t stop shaking; my entire body was vibrating. Jake put his hand on my arm, and I peeked up at him. “Breathe deep. In and out. Try to hold it as long as you can.”

I never wanted to hold my breath again, but I did what he asked. It took a few minutes, but the shaking finally stopped. The grief didn’t, and silent tears rolled down my cheeks. “They’re all gone, Jake. Every single one of them.” My voice shook as emotion tightened my throat.

“I know,” he muttered, his voice also rough with emotion. “I can’t believe this happened,” he whispered. “We weren’t supposed to be anywhere near the storm.”

Looking over at him, I swallowed the lump in my throat. "Why did you . . . why did you run into the boat for me? You could have been killed."

His brows furrowed as he stared at me. "I couldn't live with myself if you died and I hadn't done anything." His voice cracked, and he paused before continuing. "Not trying to save you wasn't an option."

"Thank you, Jake. I wouldn't have made it without you."

"I wouldn't thank me quite yet. We're not exactly in the clear," he said in response. That was definitely true. The ocean was still furious, and our little makeshift raft was rising and falling on huge swells that made me sick to my stomach. All we could do was hold on as the chilly water assaulted us and pray that we didn't fall off or tip over. God, I hoped it ended soon.

Finally, what felt like years later, the ocean calmed, and peace resumed. Jake and I relaxed against the wood, loosening our death grip somewhat. I looked around the ocean, hoping that sometime during the turmoil of the storm, another survivor had popped to the surface, but no . . . it was still just Jake and me, alone on a seemingly endless ocean with no sign of land—or help—in sight. As I glanced up at the sun continuing its descent toward the horizon, I started to fill with worry.

"What do we do now?" I asked. Had we survived a sinking ship just to die of thirst on this makeshift raft?

"I don't know," Jake said.

His words were like a blow to my heart. I'd somehow expected him to have an answer to my impossible question, like maybe all captains in training were taught about this very unlikely scenario and he'd know exactly what our next step should be. The fact that he didn't know what to do any more than I did was crushing.

We fell into an uneasy silence after that. There was nothing more to say on the subject, and we were both too shell shocked to chitchat. Either we were going to somehow be miraculously saved, or we were going to die right here, along with everyone else.

I tried not to think about it and instead focused on the now-gentle rocking motion of the ocean. Strange how something so terrifying could now be comforting. Pretending I was back on the boat, safe and sound and trying not to be nauseous, I closed my eyes and let the exhaustion take over. The need to sleep was overwhelming, and I could feel my consciousness slipping. Before I completely went under, I felt cool fingers wrap around mine. I held them tightly, never wanting to let go. A lone tear rolled down my cheek as today's events started replaying in my tired mind. I should have been dead right now, forever asleep at the bottom of the ocean. But I wasn't because of Jake, and maybe we only had a slim chance of survival, but at least we had a chance. The others didn't.

"Thank you for saving me," I murmured into the still air. I was so grateful for his presence, for his kindness. He'd always meant a lot to me, but now . . . now he was something else entirely.

Jake didn't answer me for the longest time, but just as sleep began sucking me under, I heard him say, "You're welcome, Valerie."

~

The next forty-eight hours were absolute misery. The sun pounded down on us during the day, stripping us of what precious internal water we had. My dark pants kept my legs protected, but I'd only been wearing a tank top under my chef's jacket, and my arms and face were horribly burned. Jake was suffering from the rays too. Like me, his pants kept his legs safe, but his exposed arms and face were just as battered as mine. The sun wasn't what was truly bothering me, though. It was the hunger and, even worse, the thirst. Being surrounded by water only added to the agony. My mind knew I couldn't drink the salty solution beneath me, but my body didn't care anymore. My defeated heart kept whispering, *Drink it. Maybe it will help you die faster.* Because at this point, choosing how to die seemed like my only option.

Just when I thought to broach the subject with Jake, he clasped my hand. Like he could read my thoughts—or his body was telling him the same thing—he said, "We'll make it. Don't give up."

I sighed in answer, then resumed slowly dying in silence.

Jake and I had been conserving our energy for days, barely speaking and usually resting with our eyes closed. I felt so weak, like even breathing was a struggle, and as evening settled around us, I somehow knew—I was never going to wake back up. A part of me wanted to say something to Jake, a deep and meaningful goodbye in which I admitted just how much I cared about him, how I secretly wished we had been together for the last six months, not him and my sister . . . but I was too tired to muster the words. Instead, I soaked in the beauty of the sun setting . . . memorizing its perfection, vowing to hold on to the image until the very last beat of my heart. Then I closed my eyes and quietly let sleep settle over me for the very last time.

To my absolute shock, consciousness returned to me as the warmth of the sun hit my face. A small part of me wished it hadn't; peacefully passing away in my sleep sounded glorious. I inhaled a deep, reluctant breath . . . and that was when I noticed something was different. We weren't rocking anymore.

My eyes sprang open. The blazing sun briefly stole my vision, so I shifted my focus to my ears. Waves. I could hear waves crashing, breaking against . . . something. And birds . . . birds squawking to each other. As my sight returned, I twisted my head to the side. Shock flooded through me as a seemingly endless stretch of pristine white sand filled my vision. Oh my God . . . land. I sat up quickly, and my head spun. My vision flexed and twisted, but even through the chaos, I could make out the beach underneath us, the ocean gently lapping at our feet, as if saying goodbye.

I shifted to Jake. He was still, silent. Icy fear shot through me. *God, please don't let him die now, not when we've finally made it through.* Putting my hand on his shoulder, I gently rocked him. "Jake . . . wake up."

He didn't move. He was so still I couldn't even tell if he was breathing. I shook him harder, spoke his name louder, but still nothing. Panic and fear squeezed my chest, making it hard to breathe. No, I couldn't lose him. I didn't know what I'd do without him. Not knowing what else to do, I slapped his face. His eyes instantly shot open, and he gasped in a deep, startled breath. His panicked eyes shot to mine, and I cringed. "Sorry, you weren't waking up. I thought you might have . . ."

I tried to swallow, but my throat was too dry to make the movement. Jake closed his eyes and shook his head. "Not yet," he whispered, his voice equally raw.

Glee at my discovery made me shake him again. "Jake . . . we're here. We made it."

His eyes reluctantly reopened. "Made it where?"

"Anywhere but out there," I answered, pointing to the water.

That was when Jake seemed to realize we were no longer stranded on the ocean. He bolted upright, then groaned and clutched his head. When his vision settled, he looked around at the oasis we'd stumbled upon. Then his cracked lips parted into a wide smile, and he started laughing—belly laughing. I joined him, and as I did, days of emotional agony lifted from my soul. We'd found a way to live, and I was positive that we could live here. Beyond the beach was a lush green forest. That meant water. That meant food. That meant survival.

Jake struggled to his feet. I could only make it to my knees—I'd never been so weak in all my life. My depleted muscles shook as I set one foot on the wooden raft. I groaned, cringed, and cried out in pain as I lifted my weight to standing, but I did it. And just that small feat felt like a momentous victory.

Jake grimaced, too, as he worked to get his muscles moving properly. "You okay?" he grunted.

"I will be when we find water," I told him. Just the thought of drinking made me want to cry.

A smile on his face, Jake nodded and turned to examine the landscape. As I turned to look with him, my heart sank. The island seemed huge, larger than life, since I was so desperate for nourishment. We were so close, and yet it still seemed so far. "Jake, we'll never find . . . it's too far . . ."

I wanted to sit back down; I could feel my knees buckling, threatening to do just that. I also knew getting up again would require more willpower than I had. Staying upright was a necessity, just as much as finding water.

Jake grabbed my hand, locking us tightly together, and the contact sent a much-needed jolt of adrenaline through me. The look on his face seemed to say, *You go, I go*, and I found strength in that. We were each other's buoys in this turbulent new water. I wasn't about to let him falter, and I knew he wouldn't let me falter either. "We just need water," he said. "Any source will do for now."

I nodded, then took one trudging step toward the jungle. Salvation was that way.

We entered the coolness of the forest, and I exhaled in relief as the branches shaded us from the harsh sunlight—my arms and shoulders were a shocking shade of pink, cracked and bleeding, and from the pain, I had to imagine my face was the same. After this, I seriously doubted I'd ever sit in the sun for fun again. Jake stepped away from me and began examining the ground, the bushes, the large tree leaves low enough to grab. Finally, he smiled and looked over at me. "Here, a tiny bit."

I stumbled my way over to where he was holding a gigantic leaf in his hands. In the middle of the leaf was a small pool of water, left over from a recent rainstorm. He lifted it to my lips, and I eagerly drank it down. It wasn't nearly enough to satisfy my thirst, but it gave me a surprising amount of energy. I started searching all the leaves I could, while Jake found some of his own to drink from. Several minutes later, I felt renewed. Nowhere near satiated, but to the point where I was pretty sure I wouldn't die tonight. Not from thirst, anyway.

Once Jake and I had taken every speck of water nearby that we could find, we began heading deeper into the jungle to find a more substantial supply. Traipsing through the thick foliage was grueling, and knowing that we had no idea if we were heading in the right direction or not made anxiety pulse through my veins. I was so tired, and I just wanted to rest, but the thought of filling my belly to the point of bursting with refreshing H_2O was too much of a draw to quit. I'd keep following Jake through these woods until I collapsed. Or until he did.

Plants scratched at us, leaving long, burning claw marks down our arms; thick swarms of bugs bit every inch of tender skin they could find; and the coolness on the outskirts of the jungle quickly turned to a muggy, humid, sweltering bog of heat that made beads of sweat constantly drip down my skin, dampening my clothes. I was thirsty enough that I contemplated wringing out my tank top and drinking the sweat to take back the precious moisture. But I knew, just like the ocean, sweat was far too salty. I needed cool, fresh, clean water. I needed a stream . . . just like that one.

I stopped in my tracks, staring in awe at the water flowing through the shallow creek beside me. "Jake!" I screeched, turning to look over to my right, where he was aimlessly continuing forward, deeper into the woods. He stopped when he heard my voice and looked back at me with an almost dazed expression on his face. "Water," I squealed, pointing to the ground.

He was by my side in an instant, eager to see what I'd found. The quiet brook wasn't much, but we wanted it so badly it seemed like a gushing waterfall. "You did it," Jake said, smiling at me.

I wanted to object—all I'd done was nearly stumble into the thing—but I was too desperate for a drink to be humble. Jake and I dropped to our knees and instantly began scooping the water into our hands. The heaven-sent liquid was nearly to my mouth when a thought struck me. "Is it safe to drink?" I quickly asked. I didn't want to be saved from dehydration only to die from dysentery.

Jake paused with his scooped hands to his lips. Lowering them, he studied the stream. "There's a lot of movement here . . . a lot of rocks, a lot of sand to filter out bacteria. It *should* be fine."

The word *should* didn't fill me with confidence, but in the end, it didn't really matter if the water was clean or not. We needed this, and we didn't have a way to boil it right now, so drinking it straight from the source was our only option. *Please let this be fine.*

With that wish in my head, I gulped the water down. To my delight, it didn't taste murky or stagnant. It was perfect: crisp and refreshing, just about the best water I'd had in my entire life. I was giggling in between handfuls, so grateful and happy to have something that until now, I'd taken for granted every single day of my life.

Jake watched me with a wide grin on his face, and for the first time since we'd found ourselves in this hell, his eyes shone with life, strength, and determination. It was captivating and enticing, and it made my stomach flutter with exhilarating butterflies. I was starting to feel like we might be okay after all, which brought a new realization to the surface. We'd survived the ocean, but now we were trapped on an island together. Alone. With no end to our isolation in sight. There was already so much tension between us. Would I be able to stop the attraction from growing into more? Would I be able to keep resisting him? We had to keep staying away from each other, because anything happening between us would hurt my sister. God . . . Kylie. How the hell would she get through believing she'd lost both of us? Did she already know something was wrong? Was she already worried, scared? And what about my mom and dad? Steph, Alicia, Chloe . . .

I had to forcefully shove those thoughts from my brain. Now wasn't the time to worry about our loved ones. Our survival was still too fragile.

When both of us had had our fill of water, we began carefully washing the grime and sweat from our sunburned bodies. While I was grateful for the small stream, I really wished it were a deep pool so I could cool my burning skin and bathe the filth of the last few days from me. Maybe rinse out my clothes and my hair. God, I wished I had soap. And toothpaste. And a brush. And more clothes. And pots and pans . . . and a bed. Thinking of everything we didn't have made me frown. I was pretty certain we could survive here, but how would we live?

"What is it?" Jake asked, jade eyes studying my face.

"I just . . . how are we going to do this, Jake? There's so much we don't have . . ." I shook my head as despair washed through me. "Everything. What we don't have is *everything*."

Smiling, he pointed at the stream. "Not true. We have water now. That's something we didn't have a few minutes ago. So see: our lives have already improved." He looked so chipper now that he was refreshed, but my point was a valid one.

I raised an eyebrow at his statement. "I'm serious. What do we do?"

Pressing his damaged lips together, he watched me for a moment before answering, "We follow the stream until we find a bigger source of water. That's what we do."

"But what about after that? We have no tools to build a shelter with, no weapons to hunt with; we don't even have a way to boil the water."

Keeping constant eye contact with me, Jake shook his head. "We follow the stream until we find a bigger source of water," he slowly repeated.

I let out a long exhale, then nodded. He was subtly telling me not to stress about future worries, to only focus on one action at a time. We would figure out each new problem as we came across it. But for now, we had an immediate plan, and I was going to cling to it with every scrap of hope I possessed.

Jake and I got to our feet. Jake removed his socks and washed his toes in the water, and even though it wouldn't matter the minute we started moving again, I did the same. The muddy forest floor squishing between my toes made me long for my shoes, but they were long gone . . . beginning to rot in the salty ocean. Along with . . . too many other things.

Chef Sinclair's soulless eyes flashed through my head, and my entire chest constricted with pain. *Not now. Later—I'll mourn later.* There was too much to do now. Forcing painful thoughts out of my brain, I followed Jake when he began tracking the stream. We found some strange red-and-green tropical fruit along the way. Jake handed me some, telling me that he thought they were fine to eat, and I eagerly consumed them. Thirst had been my main concern, but hunger had been gnawing a hole through my stomach for an eternity. The sweet fruit wasn't enough to fill the hole, but it did relieve a portion of the pain.

It felt like hours went by as we followed the water. Maybe it was my imagination, but the forest seemed to be getting darker, gloomier. But then we heard the telltale sound of splashing water. It was different from waves upon the shore but just as distinct. Jake turned to me, a glow in his eyes.

"Waterfall," we both said at the same time.

We rushed forward through the brush and came to a sunlit clearing. In the center of that clearing was a crystalline pool of water, begging for me to jump inside it. It backed up against a steep cliff of rock that surging water was cascading down in a never-ending sheet. Oh my God, we'd just found a faucet, bath, *and* shower.

Jake laughed as he looked around. When he turned to me, he let out a long, relieved exhale. "I think we just found our new home."

Smiling at the beautiful scene before me, I nodded. "Yes, I think we did." For better or worse, we at least had a spot to call our own now. And that fact brought me more comfort than I'd ever thought it would.

Chapter Nine

After a couple of days of floating on a small piece of decking, it was strange to have so much room to walk around. And it was even stranger to have Jake so far away from me—even if it was just a few feet. I'd gotten used to having him close enough to touch at all times. His extreme nearness had given me comfort during the dark times, when I'd been sure we'd never make it off the ocean. I'd always been insanely attracted to him, but now, I found myself desperately needing his companionship.

But we'd made it off the water, and now it was time for things to get back to normal. Well, what passed for normal here on an island. Or for us. Things had always been charged and awkward between us. What would it be like now that *we* were all there was?

"So what's first on the to-do list?" I asked, looking up at the sky, visible now, in the clearing. It had taken us a good chunk of the day to find the waterfall. A huge part of me wanted to dive right into those cerulean waters, but I knew there were more important things we should be doing right now than bathing.

"I'd love to start looking for food," Jake said, tearing his gaze from the water to look at me, "but we should start on the shelter. I'd like some sort of protection before night falls."

I nodded in agreement, then stepped back into the shade of the forest with him. Here was where we'd make camp, under the canopy of the towering trees.

Like we'd done this a million times before, Jake and I started collecting palm fronds and small branches. Jake frowned as we were working, then told me, "I'd love to cut down some of these smaller trees, use them as floorboards, but . . . no tools. Not even a pocketknife. I feel so incredibly unprepared. It's a new feeling for me, and I can't say I like it."

I gave him a soft smile, loving that little detail about him. I hadn't realized he had the heart of a Boy Scout. "It's okay. There's no way you could have been prepared for . . . what happened."

There was no way any of us could have been prepared for the intensity of the storm. Flashes of all the people who hadn't made it off the boat flickered through my mind. So many had died. I wondered how many of them had family who would be mourning them, just as our family would mourn us. God . . . Mom, Dad . . . Kylie.

Tears sprang to my eyes as I froze in place, hands still full of palm fronds. Jake noticed. "Hey," he said, his voice soft. "Don't do that."

"Do what?" I asked, tears rolling off my skin.

"Replay their deaths. Think about the people they left behind. Think about the people *we've* left behind. Whatever it is that you're doing that's making you emotional. That won't help us right now, okay?"

Exhaling all the air in my lungs, I nodded, then wiped my cheeks dry. He was right; it still wasn't time to mourn. We had too much to do. It was beginning to feel like we always would.

It took us the rest of the remaining daylight, but eventually we had enough leaves and moss that we were able to make a floor big enough for two. We placed all the greenery under a tree that had fallen during a storm and landed in the crook of another nearby tree, forming a natural ridgepole. We searched the jungle for broken branches and were lucky enough to find a dozen or so that we could use as supports for the sides of our lean-to. We drove two sturdy ones into the ground at the opening of our shelter, then used small vines to secure the other poles parallel to the inclined fallen tree. After that, we began tying on the palm fronds. When we were done, I was shocked at how cozy our new home was, and as I lay down inside it, exhaustion immediately overtook me.

Jake sat beside me. The light was fading as the day came to a close, and what remained of the sun was hidden from us by the canopy of trees and the tight packing of our palm-frond ceiling. Even still, there was enough light that I could make out his features. He was gorgeous in the twilight, and the fact that we were essentially in a bed together made nervous anticipation radiate through me. My pulse quickened as I watched him. He, however, seemed . . . pensive.

"What's wrong?" I asked. "It's not the shelter, is it? Because this place is amazing, all things considered."

He nodded, but he still looked displeased. "It will do for now, but eventually we'll need something more . . . permanent."

Right. Permanent. Because we could be here a *very* long time. Maybe for the rest of our lives.

Jake sighed as he lay down on our grassy bed. "I'll have to work on building some tools soon. Breaking rocks until they're sharp, tying them to branches . . . really primitive stuff. God, that's gonna suck. I miss my power tools already."

His comment made me smile, but it quickly fell off my face as my stomach seized in hunger. "I would give anything for some food right about now."

Jake turned his head to look at me, his eyebrows bunched in concern. "Me too. Tomorrow. We'll go scrounging for food tomorrow. Tonight, let's just try to rest . . . and not think about it."

"Sure, no problem." I'd never been this hungry in all my life, so naturally, all I could think about was food. But honestly, the physical pain—the cracked lips, the sunburned skin, the bugbites and scratches, the hollow stomach and fatigued muscles—it was all nothing compared to the emotional and psychological damage I was dealing with. "Did you ever in your life picture this happening?" I quietly asked.

Jake gave me a crooked grin. It was oddly playful, considering what I'd just asked him. "Barely surviving a shipwreck and being stranded on an island for who knows how long? No, never crossed my mind. What about you? Ever imagine this happening?"

I shook my head, then sighed. "Maybe once or twice. I've always had a bit of an irrational fear about boats." Looking over at him, I shrugged. "I might have lied about being comfortable on them. And not getting sick. I was tripling up on Dramamine, just to make it through."

Jake smiled at my admission, making butterflies dance around my stomach. "Why did you take the job, then?"

"Like you said when you told me, it was too good of an experience to miss. Sometimes you have to leap in, no matter how scared you are." I frowned at my analogy. Probably not the most appropriate one to be making right now, considering what had just happened to us. Jake only smiled at me, though, understanding what I'd meant, even if I'd said it awkwardly.

Silence blanketed us, broken only by the sound of croaking frogs and singing crickets.

"Do you think anyone will come looking for us?" I whispered.

Jake sighed as he stared off into the night. "I don't know. I'm sure they'll look for Mr. Thomas, but once they find the wreckage, I don't know that they'll comb the islands looking for survivors. They'll assume we died along with everyone else, and we'll be chalked up to two more people swept away by the current. With all the evidence pointing to us being dead, why would they endlessly search for our bodies?"

The reality of our situation began weighing me down. He was right. We could have drifted hundreds of miles away from the wreck site, and this part of the ocean was teeming with small islands. Even if someone wanted to—and why would they if they believed we were dead?—they wouldn't be able to search every island. "Kylie . . . she's going to think . . ." *That we were both dead.*

Jake let out a weary exhale, and his expression turned grim. "Yeah . . . I know."

How long would she mourn Jake before she moved on? God, here I was worried about my sister, but it was Jake who was truly going to suffer. I would never lose Kylie, no matter how long we were stuck here, but Jake . . . eventually Kylie would accept that he was gone and find someone else. He had a limited amount of time to return to her. Assuming we ever got off this rock.

"We're doomed, aren't we?" I murmured, feeling utterly defeated.

Jake gave me a half grin that he often used when he was trying to be optimistic. "No . . . not doomed. Maybe we're within sight of the shipping lanes. Maybe we'll get lucky and catch the eye of someone close enough to see us."

"And how do we do that?" I asked, incredulous. "Wave our arms?"

His small grin turned into a wide one. "No, we do it the same way people have been doing it for centuries. Fire and smoke. Tomorrow we'll go down to the beach and search for a good place to set up a bonfire beacon; then every day we'll light it . . . and hopefully we'll get lucky."

His sanguinity was adorable, but I was having a hard time sharing in it at the moment. "There's an awful lot of luck and hope involved in your strategy."

"Because that's how we'll get out of here. Luck, hope . . . and maybe a little faith."

Feeling weary for multiple reasons, I turned my head to stare at the underside of the tree branch extending over our heads. "I don't know that I believe in any of those things right now."

"You will. One day."

"And we'll probably still be here when I do believe again." Where his voice was soft and hopeful, mine was bleak and sarcastic.

Refusing to let my pessimism daunt him, he cheerily said, "At least we'll be together."

"That might not be a blessing either," I said, twisting to face him again. Every day my feelings for him were going to become stronger, more tangled around my heart. Resisting him was going to be torture. "You know how things are between us. How . . . weird . . . we can get."

Jake shook his head. "Whatever happened between us before doesn't matter now. It's a blessing we're together, Valerie. A miracle. And I'm so glad that I was able to save you. I can't imagine doing all of this alone. I can't imagine the thought of you being . . . gone." His smile slipped as that bleak thought filled him, and his eyes shimmered with pain.

Reaching out, I grabbed his hand; he wrapped his fingers around mine, holding me just as tightly as I held him. "Yeah . . . and it goes without saying, but I'm glad you saved me too. I honestly thought I was going to die down there."

His eyes flicked between mine. Grief on his face, he said, "I'm so sorry I couldn't save Chef. I swear I wanted to, but I knew he was . . ."

"I know," I said, squeezing his fingers. "And I understand why you didn't. It's okay."

His eyes drifted to the ceiling of our makeshift tent. "Letting someone die will never be okay with me."

The pain on his face hurt my soul. While I'd had to watch Chef die, Jake had had to make the terrible choice of not helping him. "Maybe not," I said, my voice soft and soothing. "But if you'd stopped to try and save him, we'd both be dead with him right now. It's a hard truth, but it's still the truth. You made the right call."

He shifted his eyes to look at me again; they were torn with pain and guilt. As much hope and faith as Jake was holding on to, he was holding on to a lot of baggage too. *My* hope was that he'd somehow find a way to release it and forgive himself. And that I could keep denying the urge to kiss away his guilt.

~

I woke up the next morning feeling so hungry I was nauseous. In fact, I was so sick to my stomach that food no longer sounded appetizing. It was similar to being so tired I couldn't sleep, only worse: I was so starved I couldn't eat. But unlike being overexhausted, I *could* force food down my throat, and I would if it came to that. Eating was too important. Of course, eating at all depended on finding food.

The space beside me was vacant when I came to full alertness. The idea of being completely alone here—lost and isolated on a deserted island—made my insides quiver with fear. I could feel panic begin to creep along the edges of my brain, trying to immobilize me, but I forced reason to override the crippling emotion. I wasn't alone. Jake was here, somewhere.

Sitting up, I listened for him in the camp, and sure enough, I heard branches snapping and leaves rustling. Poking my head out of the shelter of palm fronds, I saw Jake returning to the camp from somewhere deeper in the woods. Feeling aches in places I hadn't even known could hurt, I climbed out of the shelter to join him in the crisp morning air. He smiled as I reached his side, and a rush of joy and relief coursed through me, comforting me. It took everything I had to resist throwing my arms around him.

"So," he said, glancing back at where he'd left a clear trail through the underbrush. "I figured things would be a whole lot less awkward if we had our own private bathrooms."

"Private?" I asked, my lips curling into a mischievous grin. Privacy out here was a misleading idea. Sure, as far as we knew, we were the only ones on this island, but we couldn't exactly build a restroom with a door. And I really wished we could. This was going to be a misery for me, a hundred times worse than the boat. I kept that fact from my face, though—no reason to make any of this harder than it already was.

Jake chuckled at my question. "As private as I could out here." Pointing, he indicated the trail. "Follow that path for a bit until it forks. The left side is the ladies' room, the right side the men's. I tried to make them far enough apart that we wouldn't be able to see each other if we . . ." Frowning, he let that thought die.

I was touched that he'd even gone to that extreme, and I had a feeling it was more for my benefit than it was for his. In my experience, most men had no problems when it came to doing their business outside. It was almost a point of pride. "Thank you. That's actually a huge relief. I was a little stressed about it. Although I was going to play it off and try to be cool, because in the grand scheme of things, we've got much bigger problems."

A sigh escaped me as I examined our poor sunburned, malnourished bodies. There was so much we didn't have, starting with shoes, ending with any sort of tool. But we'd made it this far and even built a pretty decent shelter. We'd figure out the rest. We had to.

Jake ducked down to look me in the eye. "I'm going to work on tools right now. We're going to find food today, Valerie. I promise you."

The sincerity and fierceness in his jade eyes stole my breath, made my heart pound. I completely believed him. He was going to find us something to eat or die trying. I really hoped it didn't come to that last extreme. His death meant my own; I was sure of it. And just like he couldn't picture me gone, I couldn't picture him gone either. I didn't even want to. Thank God he'd made it off the boat. Thank God he'd come back for me.

After I used the island's "facilities," I headed back to camp to help Jake with tools. He wasn't there, but he'd left an arrow of sticks pointing in the direction of the waterfall. Beside it was a bunch of small rocks forming a smiley face. So cute. Laughing to myself, I followed the trampled brush leading to our plentiful source of water.

I found Jake sitting on a rock at the edge of the waterfall pool. He had a bunch of sticks and rocks around him, and he was staring at them as if willing them to turn themselves into tools he could use to save us.

"Any luck?" I asked, sitting on a rock beside him.

Shaking his head, he looked down at the mess he'd collected around his feet. "I know I've said this before, but I'd give anything for a knife."

I gave him a consolatory half smile, then examined what he'd found. Most of the rocks were just standard round rocks, but there was one that looked to have had some recent trouble. It had a deep split on the side, and a chunk looked like it was a hairsbreadth from snapping off. "What about this? If you get that edge off, it might be sharp enough to cut."

"Yeah, maybe," he said.

He grabbed the rock and went to work on breaking it into two pieces. Leaving him to his task, I headed over to the waterfall to soothe my parched throat. I couldn't stop watching him, though; the way his body moved was mesmerizing. Jake was lean in a fit, healthy way. His arms were clearly defined, like he used them often.

I studied Jake's form until finally the rock came apart in his hands. He stared at the pieces, a little dumbfounded, then thrust both hands into the air in victory. "Yes! Finally!"

His glee was contagious, and I giggled as he twisted to look at me, still standing in the water. Our eyes met, and some of the joy I felt began twisting into something else. Something a lot more primal. It didn't help anything that Jake was breathing more heavily from the exertion of breaking the rock. He was slightly sweaty, and as he wiped his brow, I suddenly wanted him to join me in the water.

I was picturing him dropping the rocks, stripping off his shirt, exposing his glorious set of abs, then walking out to the water, gripping me tight, and drawing me in for a kiss that would leave me weak in the knees. My breath hitched in anticipation as my fantasy escalated, and I was a little shocked at how badly I wanted it to happen.

That was when I finally noticed that the real-life Jake was eyeing me with a strange expression on his face. "What?" he asked, brows bunched in confusion.

Not wanting to admit just how steamy my thoughts had gotten, I averted my eyes and shrugged. "Nothing, just wondering . . . what now?" I asked, peeking back at him.

While Jake frowned and looked at his rocks, I tried to set my body straight. Not him. He was Kylie's, and once we left here, they would continue being together. They would get married, have children, build a life together . . . because that was what Kylie deserved. I needed to stop thinking about him romantically and focus on what really mattered—finding food. Actual physical sustenance.

Still examining his broken rock, Jake sat back down on his stone seat. "I think I can make this work," Jake said, glancing over his shoulder. "Thank you for the idea."

Smiling, hoping I didn't look flushed, I walked out of the water to help him with the next step, whatever that might be.

As it turned out, the next step was making multipronged spears. Jake was able to use the sharp stone to saw off some bamboo branches. Then he made cuts in the top, which I made wider by shoving twigs deep into the cracks and then tying them into place with long leaves. Within no time at all, we had four of the pointy spears.

"Ready to go fishing?" Jake asked, a pleased smile on his face.

"Hell yes," I answered.

Jake helped me to my feet, and then the two of us made our way to the ocean. We didn't take the same route we'd used when we'd first arrived. Instead, we traveled up to the top of the waterfall to see if we could get the lay of the land. Once we were at a much higher vantage point, we could see that the island was longer than it was wide, and the southerly route we'd taken to get up here was about three times as far as the beach to the west. That excited me. We were much closer to the ocean than I'd realized.

When we got down to the water, we saw that the beach here was an isolated cove. It was idyllic, like something taken right out of a travel magazine. High green hills on either side sheltered a bay of water that was the perfect shade of clean turquoise; it was so pure that I could clearly see the ocean floor for hundreds of feet around me. The beach itself was a sheet of pristine white sand, devoid of rocks and driftwood. A vacationer's dream location, and it was right in our backyard. A part of me couldn't believe that this picture-perfect beauty was ours—and only ours—for the foreseeable future. It was so flawless it was almost unreal. This was definitely my new favorite spot.

"It's gorgeous," I murmured, a little overwhelmed by the beauty of nature around me.

Jake looked over at me with a smile. "Let's hope it's full of fish too."

Hiking up our pant legs, we waded out into the water. It was surprisingly warm, like a bath. Makeshift spears in hand, we wandered out in separate directions. Divide and conquer: that was our best chance at success. The clear water made it easy to spot what was around me, and so far, that was nothing. I stepped lightly on the sandy floor, careful to not disturb the sand too much so I didn't disrupt my vision. My eyes grew weary as I studied the water for any sign of movement, and I had to remind myself to blink. I tried not to think about how vitally important our quest for food was—that just made me anxious. Instead, I pretended it was only a bit of sport, a lazy afternoon spent fishing in a refreshing cove of beautiful water. Yes, that was far less stressful.

I waded deeper into the water, until my pants were soaked to my midthigh. I instantly regretted wearing them, but taking my pants off around Jake seemed like a bad idea. I glanced over at him to see if he'd had any luck yet. He had his spear poised high like mine, ready for the attack. As I watched, he plunged it into the water. It came back empty, but it heartened me that he'd spotted something. That meant there really were fish in here.

Returning my attention to the water around me, I swept my gaze back and forth, looking for anything out of the ordinary. And that was when I spotted it—a swirl of sand and a streak of color. I drove my spear into the water, even though I knew I wasn't fast enough to catch the darting animal. My spear struck sand instead of flesh, so I quickly pulled it out again and continued the hunt.

My stomach churned with hunger as the day wore on, and as Jake and I came up empty time and time again, I tried not to let this futile attempt at fishing frustrate me. But I'd spotted—and missed—at least a dozen fish. They were so fast, so at ease in their natural environment, that catching them this way seemed impossible. We needed rods, hooks, and fishing line, or maybe a net. Anything but these caveman-like spears.

Just as I was about to yell across the cove to Jake, tell him this was pointless, I spotted movement close to me and struck. I was fully expecting to hit the ocean floor again—that was all I'd been able to hit so far—so when I felt the spear pierce something soft, I froze with shock. The water swirled with red. The vivid color jerked me back to the moment, and I yanked the spear out of the water. A brightly colored, medium-size fish was stuck to the prongs. It was a beautiful creature, and I felt guilty for ending its life, but it was food, and I was so hungry.

"Jake! I got one!"

I looked at him as he looked at me, and even from our distance, I could see his radiant smile. He pointed to the beach, and I waded back with my victory. My first of three. "You're a natural at this," Jake said when he finally gave up for the day and joined me. He hadn't managed to catch any.

"I guess they just like me," I said, small giggles escaping me. The idea of something in my stomach made me feel lighter than air.

"Understandable," Jake said, smiling warmly. "You're very likable."

Warmth rushed through me as I locked eyes with him. There was a look on his face that jolted my heart into overdrive, made my breath quicken and my nerves tingle with anticipation—pride, admiration, and something much fonder.

Tension built between us, until Jake nervously cleared his throat. "We should, uh, get back to camp," he said, indicating back into the woods. "Cook these babies up."

The sparks between us fizzled, filling me with relief. But then the realization that our battle for food was only half-won made me frown. "How do we do that? We don't have any matches."

Jake grimaced. It was an expression that didn't fill me with confidence. "We'll have to do it the old-fashioned way . . . and pray it works."

God, I was so sick of doing things the old-fashioned way. But we didn't have a choice. "Great. Lead on."

Chapter Ten

Jake trudged back to camp, and I followed him. There was a strange blend of gloom and happiness rumbling in my empty stomach. I wanted to believe we could do this—because look at everything we'd managed so far—but somehow this seemed like the hardest task of all. But on the bright side, once we were able to tackle building fires, everything else would fall into place, and life would almost seem easy again. And then maybe we could address the fact that there was fire between us, roiling under the surface. I was worried that it might explode on us if we weren't careful.

We began building a firepit when we got back to our "home away from home." Using our hands, we dug out a clean spot, then ringed it with large rocks that took forever to find. I was getting really worried about how long everything was taking—because what if lighting the fire took hours? I wanted to eat sometime today, and if it took too long, I just might eat the fish raw. Then I'd probably throw up.

Eventually we had everything we needed stacked in the firepit. All that was left was a flame. After finding a dead, dry log and a stick, Jake blew out a long breath. "Okay. Nothing to this," he said to himself. "Just work it back and forth in your palms, gently blow when there's a spark, stick it in the pocket of logs when there's a flame. No problem. You got this."

I smiled at his pep talk. "You do have this. Not a problem."

Jake gave me a half-hearted smile, then started rubbing the stick between his hands. I eagerly stared at the connection point. I think a part of me expected the magic to happen instantly. If he could actually do this, I just might tackle him in a bear hug, then kiss him all over. Maybe not. That sounded far too appealing. I would definitely give him a squeeze, though.

I stared at the moving stick so long I started falling into a trance. Disappointment began flooding me as time marched on and nothing happened. Maybe it wasn't actually possible to start a fire this way. Maybe it was all lies and false hope. Maybe we truly were doomed. No. I needed to keep the faith. This would work.

Not able to watch anymore, I decided to get the fish ready. When this did work, I wanted to be able to plop them right on the fire. Using the stone knife Jake had fashioned this morning, I removed the heads, scaled the fish, and opened up the bellies to take out the guts. It was difficult without the proper equipment, but I managed to get the job done.

I'd just finished when I heard Jake make an excited sort of squeal. "Oh God, oh my God . . ."

I looked over to see a thin stream of smoke curling into the air. As I held my breath, Jake gently blew on the scant embers he'd created through friction. I quickly said every prayer I knew. The small spark suddenly morphed into a bright flame. Jake quickly and gently laid it in the waiting hole under the logs. He blew on it some more, encouraging the tiny flame to taste the logs above it. The flame obeyed, and soon a healthy fire was licking the logs, eating its meal as voraciously as we were about to eat ours.

"Oh my God," I said, finally releasing my pent-up breath. "You did it!"

I dropped my rock knife next to the dismembered fish bodies and flung my arms around him. "You saved us, yet again," I murmured, feeling tears of relief prick my eyes as the distinct scent of a campfire filled my nose.

Jake squeezed me back, then gently pulled away to look at me. "I didn't save us alone, Valerie. You saved us too. You got the food, and without that, we'd have nothing." His praise filled me with joy and peace, and again, that feeling began swelling between us as we stared at each other. Comfort, attraction, anticipation—it was thick in the air, nearly as obvious as the smell of the smoke. Moments passed, and he was still staring at me with those penetrating green eyes, still holding me tightly. I wanted to say something, but there was nothing to say. Jake belonged with Kylie.

I timidly stepped away from him, and he awkwardly dropped his hands to his sides. Throwing on a tight smile, he exhaled a shaky breath. "Let's, uh . . . eat," he said, waving at the fire.

God, I couldn't wait to eat. And because of *us*, that was finally going to happen. I just needed to let go of the memory of his arms around me so I could focus on cooking, and that was surprisingly difficult to do. It had felt so right being in his arms.

Our dinner was the best thing I'd ever tasted. Better than any upscale restaurant I'd ever been to, better than anything I'd made with Chef Sinclair. When we were done, I finally felt satisfied. It was amazing how having food in your stomach could make everything else seem okay.

Jake let out a content sigh once he was done. "That was so good," he said, smiling over at me.

"The best," I agreed.

His smile quickly shifted to a frown. "It took forever, though. We didn't have time to set up a bonfire beacon." He glanced up at the dark treetops and sighed.

"There's always tomorrow," I said. That was one thing we had in abundance—tomorrows. But Jake was right about the fishing taking a long time. "Maybe we should split up the tasks. I'll go fishing tomorrow, while you set up the beacon."

His eyes lowered back to mine. "I guess that makes sense. You have proven to be better at it than I am." His grin turned crooked, charming. "All right, sounds good. Tomorrow I'll work on starting a really big fire. Should be fun."

Laughing at his comment, I tossed the inedible pieces of my fish into the fire. The flames were mesmerizing, the heat comforting. I felt like I could have stared into the shifting colors for hours, but the day had been surprisingly exhausting, and I was definitely ready for bed.

I excused myself to use the ladies' room, then crawled into our makeshift bed. Jake took care of the fire, then joined me. It was a little chilly after the warmth of the fire, and I found myself scooting into his body, my entire side touching his entire side. I wished he would put his arm around me, pull me in close. Purely for his body heat. Okay, not for that reason. Even though I knew it was wrong, I craved a connection to him, longed for contact. But that road just led to heartache. And I had enough aches at the moment.

With a sigh, I turned onto my side, away from him.

"Good night, Valerie," he said into the quiet of the night.

Even though I didn't want it to happen, my lips curled into a smile, and I inched my back closer to his. "Good night, Jake."

~

I almost felt normal in the morning. Even more so when I finally realized I could do the one thing I'd been wanting to do for a long time. "After fishing, I'm going to take a bath," I stated, a bright smile on my face.

"Be careful," Jake responded, a crease on his brow. "We don't know what types of wild animals are on this island with us."

"I will, but I think it will be fine. It's not that far from camp, and so far, we haven't come across anything on this trail."

"Yeah, but I thought I heard pigs last night."

My grin widened. "Pigs? Like bacon?" That sounded amazing.

He grinned at my enthusiasm, but it quickly fell off him. "Wild pigs are actually quite dangerous. You don't want to come across a group of them without protection." He rubbed his jaw as he thought. "I should make some spears out of stone, just in case." He paused to nod. "Yeah, I'll do that after making the bonfire."

He seemed excited to get started on his day, eager to be doing something useful. I wondered if that was because of the situation, or if he was just a genuinely productive guy. There were things about Jake I just didn't know yet . . . things my sister probably knew. But I supposed now was as good of a time as any to find out.

"So how do you know about all of this survival stuff anyway?" I asked as I sat on a rock beside him.

He cringed as he looked up at me. "Does it seem like I know what I'm doing? I suppose that's good, but I'll be honest—I'm winging it."

That wasn't exactly the answer I'd wanted to hear, but I had to give him points for being honest. And "winging it" was working so far; we'd made it through some pretty dire situations.

Jake shrugged as he watched my reaction. "I've always been pretty good at problem-solving, and I watch a lot of documentaries on stuff like this."

I raised an eyebrow at that. "TV? That's how you're keeping us alive?"

He grimaced again, and I laughed. Lightly laying a hand on his arm, I told him, "So long as it works, it doesn't matter where you learned it."

Jake silently studied me, his smile warm, his eyes soft. The look on his face pulled at something inside me, an ache for attention, a need to feel appreciated and desired by him. It was getting harder to ignore the ache, but for the sake of my sister, I had to.

Removing my hand from his warm skin, I told him, “I should go get started on that fish. I do *not* want to go hungry again. That sucked.”

Jake made a jerking motion, like he’d been under a spell and was suddenly snapping out of it. The reaction made a flicker of that ache return, but I forcefully squashed it down. Jake shifted his gaze to the dormant fire. “Yeah, I should go too.” His eyes returned to mine. They were concerned this time. “Please be careful, okay?”

I gave him a smile as I stood up. “Always.”

After leaving his side, I made my way to the lagoon. I thought I’d be trying to spear some food all day, but it went easier this time. I was getting better already. Once I had enough fish for us to eat for the day, I went back to camp. Jake was gone, working on the bonfire, presumably. Even though we were in the middle of a forest, camp was quiet without him. Lonely.

I wanted to go bathe, but I really had no idea what to do with the fish. I couldn’t exactly hold them all day. Underneath something heavy seemed the safest place for them, so I wrapped them in some large leaves, then stacked a bunch of rocks on top of them in a pyramid shape. That wouldn’t keep out truly hungry animals, but maybe they’d still be there when I returned from the waterfall.

When I got to the picturesque pool around the gushing waterfall, I instantly began stripping off my clothes. The fresh water was calling my name. I paused before ripping off my shirt and instinctively looked around. With the way things often were between Jake and me—with the longing gazes and anticipatory tension—I didn’t want to be caught getting naked by him.

From the edge of my vision, I saw something odd in the sky. Smoke. A lot of smoke. I smiled as I realized that meant Jake had successfully lit a bonfire beacon. The chances of anyone seeing it were dreadfully low, but it did give me a surprising amount of hope. At least we were trying.

Feeling better knowing exactly where Jake was, I tore off my shirt and then the rest of my clothes. I tiptoed into the water, carrying my clothes with me. Maybe I could try washing some of the grime off against some rocks. Not a great solution but better than nothing. The water was freezing, much colder than the relatively warm ocean water, but it was a hot, humid day, and it felt wonderfully refreshing against my bare skin. When the water was up to my waist, I held my breath and sat down, taking my clothes with me. My entire body being enclosed in the frigidness made a small squeal escape me, but then I sighed and relaxed back into the water. It was heaven.

I took some time to attempt to clean my clothes with large rocks on the bottom of the pond. It didn't make much of a difference, but I felt like they were cleaner. After wading over to the shore, I set them on some rocks to dry, then dived under the water and swam to the deepest part. I ran my fingers through my hair as I floated on my back, washing away the sweat, grime, and leaves. I instantly felt more human.

After relaxing for a few moments, curiosity began to eat at me. Could I stand directly beneath the waterfall? Use it as a shower? I swam over there but soon discovered it was too deep. Wondering how deep it was, I dived under the surface, hands outstretched, searching for the bottom. I didn't touch the ground, but I did feel something . . . odd. Almost branch-like, but harder, like stone. Maybe it was something Jake could use as a tool. Making spears out of stone sounded awful. Grabbing the odd material, I tried to surface. I couldn't. The thing was stuck. I resurfaced for some air, then tried again.

This time, I felt more of the oddly hard, thin material. I felt up the strange surface until I felt something that was soft and felt strangely like . . . clothes. My eyes shot open as panic flared up my spine. The water was murky here, dark from the depths and the swirling mud from the waterfall current above me, but I could clearly make out the silhouette of a skeleton.

Priding myself on not screaming, I shot up to the surface, then swam far away from the long-dead body.

"Valerie? You okay? You look freaked out."

I jerked my head around to where Jake was standing at the edge of the pond, some stout branches in his hand. For a moment, surprise that he was here—while I was naked—made me forget my discovery. My heart started pounding, and an odd desire to have him with me absorbed my every thought. Shaking my head, I forced aside the feeling and told him what I'd found. "There's a body in the water. An old one."

His eyes widened in surprise, then narrowed in disbelief. "Really? Are you sure?"

He dropped his branches . . . then stripped off his shirt. It was hard to keep treading water as his bare body suddenly came into view. Sweet Jesus, I hadn't been ready to see him half-naked again in all his defined-ab glory. And that tattoo . . . he was too far away for me to read it, but the sexiness of the script was making me feel overheated. "What are you doing?" I sputtered.

"I'm going to go look at the body." He paused, like he'd just now realized I wasn't wearing any clothes. "I won't look at you . . . I promise."

I swam to the edge of the pool, where it was shallow enough that I could sit on my knees, then crossed one arm over my chest while pointing with the other to where I'd discovered the skeleton. "It's over there, deep down."

As Jake began removing more of his clothes, I began to believe that he was going to strip down to his birthday suit. I would not be able to politely ignore that, and my reaction would probably be undignified and embarrassing. Thankfully, though, he left his underwear on. They fit him perfectly, like he could be a model for the brand.

Jake strolled out to the deeper section of the water, then dived under the surface, heading to the spot I'd indicated. He seemed completely natural as he swam under the water, like he was part fish. It was mesmerizing to watch him move, and I stared at his body until he went too deep for me to see him. He was down there for quite a while, long enough for me to get worried about him. I was pushing away from my safe spot, on my way to go rescue him, when he finally popped to the surface. I was deep enough now that I had to tread water, but I still let out a relieved sigh when I saw he was okay. "Did you find it?" I said above the sound of the waterfall.

Jake grinned in answer. "I did. And that's not all I found . . ." He lifted his hand to show me a sturdy-looking knife held tightly in his fist.

Joy and relief surged through me so fast I felt light headed. God, a knife. Such a simple item, but so vastly important to us. Jake swam my way, then handed it to me. With his body so close to mine, I suddenly became acutely aware of not having any clothes on. Damn it. Why hadn't I left on my underwear, like him?

Keeping his promise to not look at my nakedness, Jake kept his eyes glued to my face. So sweet. "The guy's boots seemed to be in good shape still, all things considered. I'm going to see if I can pull them up."

"Why is there a skeleton in the water?" I asked before he could swim away. "Where did he come from?"

Jake pursed his lips as he treaded water. "He looked military to me . . . World War II, probably. These islands were stopping points for all sorts of missions. Maybe we got lucky, and this island was important back then. Maybe we'll find more stuff we can use."

"Like a boat?" I asked, grinning.

Jake laughed, looking happier than I'd ever seen him look. Then he twisted around and dived under the surface, giving me a pretty decent shot of his backside before he disappeared.

While he was trying to retrieve a dead soldier's boots, I took the opportunity to swim back to my clothes and hurriedly re-dress. I was soaking wet and my things were still damp, but it felt good to be covered again. And armed. I clutched the knife to me with a wide smile, so happy for the tool fate had dropped in our laps.

I was even happier a few minutes later when Jake sloshed out of the water carrying a pair of soggy black boots. They were in desperate need of drying and looked like they were barely holding together, but we'd both been walking around barefoot since we'd arrived here. Even if we had to rip off the rubber soles and tie them to our feet with vines, it was better than nothing.

"Oh my God, Jake," I said when he reached my side. "This is amazing! Do you really think there could be more things like this out there?"

He nodded, his grin unrestrained. "Yeah, where there's one body, there's probably more. A lot of those island skirmishes were bloody." His smile fell some. "Which is horrible, but at the moment, you know . . ."

"It's kind of a lifesaver. Yeah. We should go hunting for things, as soon as possible." There were so many potential treasures out there, and all we had to do was look for them.

Jake nodded again, then set the boots on a nearby rock to dry. "Let's eat first." He glanced down at his mostly naked body, and my eyes inadvertently followed. "And maybe dress and dry off . . . ," he finished, grabbing his slacks.

A nervous tittering laugh escaped me as he pulled them on. "Right . . . clothes . . . ," I murmured. As he dressed, my eyes drifted over his body, settling on his tattoo. The script said, *Believe you can and you're halfway there*. God . . . that was one of my favorite quotes: inspirational, motivating, reminding me that I could be whatever I wanted to be. Seeing it emblazoned on his skin made it my absolute favorite quote of all time. I had to bite my lip as he finished dressing, and a small sigh escaped me when his stomach was covered again.

Once Jake was dressed, we headed back to camp to eat some of the fish I'd buried. There was a buoyancy in the air and a lightness in our step that hadn't been there before. This new discovery was filling us with some much-needed cheer. We were more relaxed as we sat around the fire eating the thankfully undisturbed fish, and we smiled a lot more. In fact, I found myself staring at Jake more and more frequently, memorizing him, admiring him, imagining the perfect pecs I knew he was hiding under his shirt, the tattoo I longed to trace with my fingers . . .

I knew it wasn't the proper thing to be picturing, but the more I watched him, the more I wanted to watch him. It felt so natural. So right. And it wasn't one sided. Jake was watching me just as much as I was watching him. Our eyes locked frequently during our meal. Even though it was wrong, I didn't want it to end. Things were so quiet here, so isolated, so beautiful. It made the real world seem distant, almost like it no longer existed or like we were stuck in a dream. I had to keep reminding myself that this wasn't a fantasy . . . and Jake wasn't mine.

Once our meal was finished, Jake stood from the rock he was using as a chair. "Well," he said. "Want to get started on our treasure hunt?"

He extended his hand to help me stand, and I grinned as I grabbed it. "Absolutely. Where should we start, though? This island is huge."

Twisting, Jake faced where the waterfall was located. "I thought maybe we'd go back to the top of the waterfall. If the body washed down from up there, then we might get lucky."

"Sounds perfect," I murmured, studying his strong jawline.

Turning back to me, Jake smiled, then picked up the knife. "We'll mark the trees as we go so we know how to get back."

For the millionth time, I was so grateful that he was here. I probably wouldn't have thought of that little detail, and I'd probably have ended up getting horribly lost.

Jake put on his newly rescued boots, grimacing a bit as he pressed his toes inside. "They're still pretty wet, but it's better than nothing." He glanced at my bare feet and frowned.

I held up a hand to reassure him. "I'll be fine. And besides, we're probably going to find another set today, right?"

A half grin graced his lips. "You're starting to sound as optimistic as me. I like it."

And I like you. More than I should. Not wanting to ruin the good feeling in the air, I left my thoughts unspoken, but that was getting harder and harder to do.

Chapter Eleven

We hiked back up to the top of the waterfall, Jake holding my hand whenever the terrain got tricky. I found that I really liked the skin-to-skin contact, and whenever the path was clear, I wished for hills and large rocks that he had to help me over. Any excuse to touch him.

There was a rushing stream at the top of the falls, but that was it. No pile of bodies, no weather-worn clothes to sift through. Nothing. I was both relieved and disappointed. I glanced Jake's way, and he had the same conflicted expression on his face.

"This is weird, isn't it?" I asked him.

He looked over at me with a sheepish smile on his face. "Definitely. Hoping for dead bodies wasn't something I'd ever imagined myself doing." Reaching out, he grabbed my hand. It sent a zing of electricity up my spine. I knew I should avoid unnecessary intimacy, but I really loved it when he touched me. "I know I've said it before, but I'm really glad you're here. It makes all of this a little more . . . bearable."

His sentiment made me grin, made a flutter of nerves tickle my stomach. "Yeah . . . I know. It's horrible but wonderful too." I instantly clamped my mouth shut after I said that. I shouldn't say stuff like that. The situation was strange and awkward enough.

Jake looked guilty as he glanced down at his feet. I could feel his hold on my hand loosening. Not wanting him to let go yet, I squeezed him harder and pointed with my free hand at the lush landscape. "So should we start looking around? If there are bodies up here, nature has probably done a good job reclaiming them."

Jake slightly shook his head, like he was shaking away his conflicted feelings. Then he nodded. "Yeah, you're right. Of course they wouldn't just be lying out in the open. That war was decades ago. We'll need to dig around." He grimaced, like he wasn't looking forward to that. Honestly, I wasn't, either, but the end result would be worth it.

We began systematically searching around the stream, rummaging through the underbrush, looking for unnatural clumps of greenery. Anything that might indicate something buried underneath. We didn't find any bodies, but we did find sources of food in our search—berry bushes, coconut trees, banana plants. Finding other things to eat besides fish was remarkably invigorating. By the time we called it a day and stumbled to bed, we were both tired but satisfied. All in all, it had been a good day. And as I lay close to Jake's side, falling asleep, I allowed myself to rest my hand on top of his. And when he flipped his hand over so our fingers could interlace, a peaceful smile spread over my lips. Maybe it wasn't so bad here after all.

~

Over the next several days, Jake and I developed a routine on the island. After waking up, I'd go fishing while Jake tended to the bonfire. We'd meet up for lunch and eat whatever I'd caught or foraged, and then we'd go searching for dead soldiers. It was morbid but busying work, and the days seamlessly flowed into one another.

Every morning I looked forward to the day's activities, and every evening I looked forward to crawling into bed with Jake. Even though I missed my friends and family like crazy and I couldn't wait to get back to them, I kind of loved our new life. I thought Jake was beginning to love it, too, until one morning when I woke up to see him staring aimlessly at our makeshift firepit. The look on his face wasn't a content one. He looked on the verge of breaking down.

"Hey, you okay?" I asked, creeping out of our shelter to sit beside him.

He smiled at me, but I could tell it was forced. "Sure."

I pursed my lips at his answer. "No, really. Are you okay?"

The smile fell off his lips with a sigh. "I don't know. It's just . . . it's been three weeks." He pointed to a tree nearby, where he'd been making a hash mark every morning to mark the passage of time. I'd been purposely avoiding looking at the "calendar." I didn't want to know.

"Oh," I murmured, a little shocked at how much time had passed. Being on the island was like stepping outside of time. It made it easy to forget that back home, the chaos of life was continuing without us.

Green eyes locked on the tree, Jake shook his head. "They know by now. And they've accepted it. They all believe we're dead. Kylie believes I'm . . ." Swallowing a lump in his throat, he looked over at me. "Do you think she's okay?"

Hot tears pricked my eyes. This was why I hadn't wanted to look at the tree. I didn't want to think about Kylie, think about my friends, think about my parents, think about everyone's pain. Pain I'd caused them. Pain *we'd* caused them. I shook my head. "No," I said in answer. There was no way my sister was okay. She was devastated. Sobbing. Heartbroken on multiple levels. *God, I'm so sorry, Kylie.*

Jake nodded, then hung his head. I wrapped my arms around his shoulders, hugging him, comforting him. I held him for long, silent seconds until finally he said, "Even though she thinks I'm . . ." He looked up and searched my eyes. "How long do you think I have before she . . . moves on? How long do I have before I lose her?"

There was so much anguish on his face, so much grief in his eyes. It killed me to see the pain he was feeling because of another woman, but I understood why he was hurting. I swallowed the lump in my throat.

"I don't know . . . right now she's grieving, mourning you, and she's in too much pain to even think about dating someone else. That could last months, maybe even years. I know if it were me, it would take forever to move on from losing you." My eyes drifted over his hauntingly gorgeous face. "You're not the kind of person someone gets over quickly . . ."

I cringed as my heart leaked into my words. I hadn't meant to put real feeling into that, but I hadn't been able to stop myself. Jake's expression morphed into one of compassion. "Valerie, I—"

Not wanting a tender moment to pass between us right now, when I felt so weak and vulnerable, I shot up off the rock I was sitting on. "I think I'm going to take my bath early today. Don't go to the waterfall for a while, okay?"

I felt a little better after cleaning up. At times, it was so wonderful being here with Jake that my heart felt like it was about to burst with joy. Other times—when I remembered he wasn't mine—it was so painful and awkward that I wanted to be anywhere but here on the island. If only I knew what our future was going to be. Would we be rescued? Or would we be stranded here forever?

When I got back to camp, Jake was gone. Probably tending the bonfire. We lit it every day in the hopes that someone would see it, but so far we hadn't spotted any ships on the seemingly endless ocean, and no one had spotted our signal. Being lost with no effective way to communicate with the outside world was a horrible feeling.

Now that Jake wasn't in the area, I felt guilty for bolting on him. He'd needed comfort, and I'd failed him. Sure, I'd given him a little bit of support, but it hadn't felt like enough. He'd clearly needed . . . more, and I hadn't been there for him.

I looked around the shelter, feeling truly alone for the first time in weeks. This place looked a lot different than it had our first night here. Once Jake had found the knife in the water, he'd gone to work making this place better. Our shelter was still an A-frame shape, but we had a wooden floor now and much sturdier sides. He'd also carved bowls, spoons, forks, and several other everyday essentials that we hadn't had before. He was quite talented at making things; our camp felt almost like a home now.

I shifted to look over at Jake's calendar tree, letting the weight of time settle over me. Three weeks. Three weeks of sleeping side by side every night, three weeks of keeping each other company, three weeks of keeping each other alive. It had felt shorter than that, but at the same time, it had felt so much longer. The attraction we'd both felt coming onto the island had only grown while being here. I'd started this journey being hopelessly allured by him, but now . . . now I was positive I was in love with him. He was everything I'd ever wanted in a man and more. But it didn't matter, because he wasn't mine. He belonged with Kylie.

Knowing I couldn't just stand here all day and contemplate my tangled heart, I picked up my spear and prepared myself to catch some dinner. I was just about to head out on the well-worn trail when I heard the sound of something crashing through the woods toward me. Fear instantly slammed into my body, freezing my nerves. What sort of animal could make that much noise? The wild pigs Jake had heard a while back? We'd never spotted them, only signs of their existence throughout the jungle, and from everything Jake had told me about how dangerous they were, I knew I didn't want to run into them alone. I swung my fishing spear around in front of me, just in case. It was a weak weapon against a pig, too flimsy to make much of a difference to their thick hides, but at least it was something.

My palms grew sweaty as the sound of snapping twigs grew louder. God, whatever it was, it was huge. I ducked down in my stance, lowering my center of gravity. Whatever was coming, it wouldn't take me without a fight. I held my breath while I waited for the animal to break through the denser brush into this small clearing. When it finally crashed through, it took me a moment to understand what I was seeing.

"Jake?" I'd been so convinced that a charging animal was nearly upon me that his presence was baffling. "What's going on?" He was panting, hands on his knees as he caught his breath.

He smiled, then noticed my stance and surprise. "Sorry, didn't mean to scare you. I just had to tell you what—"

Instantly understanding, I interrupted him. "Oh my God, a ship! There's a ship, and it saw our signal?"

His expression dampened as he stood up straighter. "Uh, no . . . sorry. Didn't mean to get your hopes up either."

"Oh . . . then what is it?"

His mood instantly perked back up. "You're going to have to see it to believe it." He extended his hand to me, and I set down the spear and grabbed it. The joy on his face was contagious, and it instantly obliterated the odd moment we'd had this morning. I couldn't wait to see what he wanted to show me.

"Okay." I grinned, eager to be off on an adventure with him.

Nearly bouncing with excited energy, he turned us back toward where he'd burst into camp, and then he quickly began moving us away. Even though we weren't quite running, it wasn't long before I was breathing more heavily and starting to sweat. A part of me wanted to ask him to slow down, but I didn't want to dull his eagerness. Or my own. What the heck had he found?

He stopped us in front of a moss-covered wall of rock. God, we didn't have to climb that, did we? Because I really didn't think I had the energy at the moment. Jake was staring at me with that little-boy smile on his face, like he expected me to see something in the greenery. "I don't . . . what are we looking at, Jake?"

My gaze was still focused up, at the top of the massive boulder. Jake grabbed my chin, redirecting my eyes to the boulder itself. I wanted to instantly understand what he was trying to show me, but the intimacy of his hand on my face was too much; I suddenly couldn't focus on anything else.

Sadly, he let go of my face, then swept his hand toward the boulder. "See anything strange?"

"No, it's just a rock."

"Look again," he softly said, leaning toward me.

It was difficult to think with him so close, but I tried my best to ignore his presence and concentrate on the rock. I didn't want to look like an idiot by not being able to see what he apparently thought was obvious. "I don't . . . wait . . ." Finally seeing something odd, I stepped toward the wall. "Is that . . . a door?"

What I'd thought was just a huge boulder was much too flat to be a natural rock, and directly in the center of the rock wall, there was a rectangular outline, clearly indicating a door. And beneath it, on the ground, there was an arched line of scraped debris, from where the door had recently been opened. Oh my God . . .

"Yes!" Jake exclaimed. "It's a bunker. It's been so consumed by the forest that I've missed it every day as I walked by here, but I noticed it today, and yeah, you're not going to believe this. Close your eyes," he said with a grin.

I frowned at his need for a dramatic reveal, but I did what he asked. I heard the door groaning open, like the thick metal still wasn't used to moving. Once the sound stopped, I felt Jake grab my hand. I clutched him tight, excited, nervous, and loving his touch. He started pulling me forward, and I took small, careful steps. Even still, I stumbled a little on the edge of the door. Jake steadied me, reaching around behind me to grab my elbow. His chest was pressed against my back, and I could feel his thundering heartbeat. Or maybe that was just mine.

Not really wanting the sensual moment to end, I asked, "Can I open my eyes now?"

"Not yet," he said in my ear. Then he left my side. I instantly frowned at the loss of our connection but waited patiently until he told me he was ready. I heard a match light, then the whoosh of kerosene igniting. Were there lamps down here? This was already amazing.

"Okay . . . go ahead and open them."

I did so slowly, cautiously, like I was either nervous or savoring the moment. Maybe a little of both. My mouth dropped open when I saw just what he'd been so excited to show me. Steep stairs led down to where the bulk of the bunker was carved into the earth. It was a huge room filled with supplies and commodities—everything we'd need to make it here. And with just a quick glance, it seemed like there were enough supplies to last us a few years, especially with only the two of us consuming them.

"Oh my God," I murmured, wandering down the steps to enter the main living space of the bunker.

"I know, right?" Jake said, following me with the lamp. "It's incredible. Everything we need."

Shelves lined two walls of the room. They were packed full of canned goods, clothes, blankets, toiletries, tools, and gear, including actual fishing poles and a couple of axes. Jake set the lamp down on a table, and I marveled that there was a table. That was when I noticed that there was a kitchen, complete with pots, pans, and a kerosene stove. I could actually cook a decent meal again.

Jake was grinning as he watched me. Then he pointed over to a section of the room I hadn't looked at yet. "Oh my God, there's a bed!" There was only one, and it looked like it was on the small side, but it had a mattress, and after weeks of us sleeping on hard surfaces, it seemed like the most luxurious thing on earth. I squealed as I ran over and flopped on top of it. The springs squeaked, and the pillow and blanket smelled musty, but even still, it was heaven.

"Wow," I murmured, my eyes watering with emotion. "You wouldn't think a bed could make a person cry, but yeah, I think I'm about to lose it."

I sat up on the bed, and Jake grinned wider as he sat beside me. "I know what you mean. I already did."

"Jake, this is . . . this is a game changer. I'm so happy you found this place." *Happy* didn't seem like the right word. *Ecstatic*, *thrilled*, *overjoyed* . . . those were much more accurate, but they felt too silly to say. I didn't need to say them, though. Jake knew; he understood. This bunker was life. There was absolutely no question that we were going to be okay now that the urgency of surviving had been depleted somewhat. Now we could truly focus on being rescued, on going home. It was a new era for us on the island, and it was all thanks to Jake—I never would have spotted this place.

"You're amazing," I said, putting a hand on his arm.

Jake glanced down at my fingers, then back up at my face. "I'm not the only one," he murmured.

The warmth in the air seemed to grow as we stared at each other, and my heart began to race with anticipation. The way he was looking at me was beyond friendship, beyond admiration. His entire soul was showing in his jade eyes, drawing me in, making me long to connect with him. Was it just this morning that he'd seemed so desolate over the fact that he was slowly losing my sister? Because he sure didn't seem that way now.

The tension in the air grew even higher, and my heart began to race. I wasn't sure who started the movement first, but before I knew it, we were both moving toward each other. My eyes drifted to his lips just as his fingertips touched my cheek. God, I'd dreamed about this for so long. But even still, it wasn't right. I should stop it from happening.

But before I could gather the strength to move away, our lips connected, and my breath completely stopped. A flicker of guilt washed through me, but it was instantly swept away by a tidal wave of desire. Months. I'd wanted this man for months. His mouth gently moved against mine while his hand cupped my cheek. I felt like I was floating or dreaming or stuck in some other reality, one I never wanted to leave.

Only I had to . . . because he wasn't mine.

Kylie. She loves him; she needs him. And there's still hope for them . . . if we're found soon.

Guilt and loyalty made me break away from his lips. I searched his eyes. "We should stop."

My words instantly snapped him out of his trance. He shot up off the bed and ran a hand through his messy hair. "God, Val, I'm sorry. I just . . . I got carried away. I didn't mean to . . ."

"It's okay," I said. "It's just . . . not a good idea. We could be picked up at any time, and you and Kylie . . ."

Jake scrubbed his hands over his eyes. "I know; I'm sorry. This island, all the stress . . . and you, you're so goddamn . . . everything was already so confusing, and now it's just . . . so much worse." He sighed as he looked at me. "I honestly don't know what's going on with me anymore, and I'm so sorry if I'm hurting you. I don't mean to."

"It's okay," I repeated, a little dazzled by what he'd said.

He shook his head. "No, it's not. It's not fair. We're just supposed to be friends, but I keep pushing against that line." Giving me a reluctant smile, he shrugged and said, "I'll do better to not be such a sucky friend. I promise."

I could only give him a tiny, awkward grin in response, since a part of me didn't want him to just be my friend anymore. I just had to keep suppressing that part of me. Then we'd be fine.

Chapter Twelve

Life was so much easier in the bunker. Now that we weren't struggling to survive every second of every day, we had time to talk, time to play. The break from the extreme did wonders for our mental health. Not to mention the fact that we were getting a good night's sleep every evening now, although sleeping in a small bed with Jake brought its own problems—especially after that kiss, a kiss that haunted my dreams.

Jake was keeping his word and just being friendly, but it wasn't stopping me from falling even harder for him. If anything, it just made it worse. He was such a good person, and being alone with him for all this time but forcing myself to not act on my feelings was torture. Sheer torture.

But we were making it through, and time was speeding up on us. Before I knew it, Jake's new makeshift calendar that he'd scratched on the wall in chalk had us on the island for three whole months.

"Wow, three months. I can't believe it's been that long already," Jake murmured, making a new hash mark.

"Yeah . . ." And we were no closer to being rescued. We'd been lighting that damn fire every day, and not one single ship had passed by. "You know, Jake, it might be time to consider the fact that we aren't getting off this island."

He snapped his gaze to mine, annoyance and reluctance on his face. He didn't want to admit that, not even to himself. "It hasn't really been all that long. Not in the grand scheme of things."

I nodded and didn't argue my point further. He wasn't ready. And maybe he was right. Three months wasn't all that long.

After a hearty fish-soup breakfast, Jake went down to the beach to light the fire. I debated joining him, going fishing, or going to our watering hole/bathtub. In the end, I decided on a nice relaxing swim.

It was a bit more of a hike to get to the waterfall now, but I didn't mind. It helped to clear my head, if not my heart. It started lightly sprinkling while I walked, and I found the cool droplets refreshing. Maybe I'd visit our old camp today, relive the "hard" days. Or maybe I'd spread out my towel and lie out in the sun—something I'd never thought I'd do again.

Just as I was weighing my options, the sprinkling turned into a decent rainfall. It was enough to make me stop in my tracks and look up at the sky. I was deep in the forest, but the rain was heavy enough to penetrate the canopy and start to soak me. Giving up on all my ideas, I tossed the towel over my head and headed back home to the bunker.

It was a monsoon-level downpour by the time I got there. "Jake, you in here?" I said, drying off my hair as I walked down the steps. "It's so crazy outside. I'm glad we moved." Pausing my hands, I looked around the very empty bunker. "Jake?" Was he still outside in that mess? I couldn't imagine he was still trying to light a bonfire in this. It would never ignite.

I set down the towel and made my way to the door. The rain was loud when I opened the door; it reminded me of a rock concert. The wind had picked up, too, and the trees around the entrance were being bent at vicious angles. It was getting bad out there, and for some reason, Jake was still in the thick of it. "Jake?" I yelled, knowing he probably wouldn't be able to hear me through this noise.

Every second that passed, the storm seemed to worsen. If he wasn't back yet, there was a reason for it. He was hurt and alone and about to be stuck in some crazy tropical storm. He'd risked everything to save me from the ship; I couldn't abandon him in his hour of need. Mind made up, I closed the door on our shelter and headed back out into the woods to find him.

The wind flicked my hair around my head, and the rain made it sting like thousands of tiny whips. Within a minute my clothes were soaked, and I was shivering as more icy drops assaulted me. I wanted nothing more than to be back in our warm, safe home, but there was no way I was going back without Jake. I kept calling his name, hoping he'd hear me somehow. Overhead, lightning crackled in the sky, and mere seconds later, thunder reverberated through the heavens. Damn, it was close. Outside was not the place to be right now.

"Jake!" The ground around me was slick with mud and running water. I had on shoes that we'd found in the bunker, but they weren't providing enough traction, and I kept slipping. More than once, I had to grab onto the branches around me to stop myself from falling on my ass.

"Jake!" I repeated, feeling desperate. God, where was he? The storm was so loud I couldn't even hear the ocean. What if I was going the wrong way? What if I got lost out here in this mess? So many things could go wrong right now, but I couldn't stop, couldn't turn back. I had to find him. "Jake!"

"Valerie?"

His voice was quiet under the wind, but I heard it and spun in that direction. "Jake! Where are you?"

"Over here! Down the ridge!"

I spun again until I saw the hill he was talking about. I carefully ran to the edge of it and looked down. Jake was on the ground there, pants covered in mud, holding his leg as he tried to stay as much out of the storm as he could. "Hey," he said, looking up at me. "What brings you to this neck of the woods?"

"You," I said, a relieved laugh escaping me. "What happened?"

He indicated the muddy trail beside him. "Slipped coming up. I think I tore something. I can't put any weight on my ankle."

Well, crap. How would I get him home, then? He was way too heavy for me to lift. "Okay, hold on . . . I'm coming down to you." As carefully as I could, I made my way down the slippery trail to him.

He cringed as I sat beside him. "It really frickin' hurts." He let out an annoyed sigh. "I'm sorry you had to come get me in this." He tilted his head up to the rain; he was just as soaked as I was and was shivering just as badly. We both needed to get out of here; the only question was how.

"Don't worry about that. Let's just get you home." I looked around the jungle, hoping against hope that I'd find something I could use. Or maybe a friendly gorilla who'd kindly offer to lend a hand. Not likely.

"Hey," he said, bringing my attention back to him. "Just leave me here and get back to safety." As if to punctuate his point, the lightning crackled again. And again, it was instantly followed by thunder.

"No way," I told him. I couldn't sit in our nice, warm home knowing he was out here suffering. "I'm getting you out of here." One way or another.

I started looking around again, hoping to be inspired by something. Cool fingers touched my cheek, turning me back to him. "Valerie, please. Leave me." Jake's eyes were wide, worried . . . for me, not him.

"No," I sputtered. "We survive *together*. You remember that?"

He shook his head. "I won't be responsible for you getting hurt."

"And I won't leave you to die."

"I won't die. I'll be fine. Valerie, please . . ." His hand on my face clenched me tighter. "Please go."

My heart was racing as I stared at him, his green eyes wide with worry, his lips wet with rain. Every instinct inside me told me the situation was dire, that I should be doing something to help him, but all I could focus on was his face. "I'm not leaving you," I whispered. "I'll never leave you . . ."

His face softened as he stared at me. "Valerie . . . I . . ." His eyes drifted to my mouth while his hand shifted to my neck. My mind had just a fraction of a second to comprehend what was happening as I felt him pull me toward him. I went willingly, eagerly.

Our mouths met, cool from the rain. My pulse was pounding in my veins as we moved together. I could hear myself whimpering with need as the storm raged on around us—thunder and lightning rattling the heavens. Jake's hand tightened in my wet hair, pulling me in deeper. His tongue brushed against mine, and every nerve ending in my body charged to life. I wanted him, so much. But I needed to get him to safety. That took precedence over physically connecting with him.

I broke away from his passionate kiss to see his eyes blazing with need. Then he blinked, and realization made his expression completely change. "Oh God, I'm so—"

I cut him off with a shake of my head. "Not now. We need to get home. It's getting bad out here." Lightning crackled in the sky, as if to punctuate my point.

Jake glanced at the sky, then nodded. "Okay . . . but how?" he asked, still looking guilty and confused.

How. That was a good question. "How's your other leg?" I asked him. "Maybe if you use me as a crutch, you'll be able to hobble your way back?"

Shrugging, he said, "I don't really see any other options at this point. I still think you should just leave me, though."

"Not a chance." I smiled, squatting down to help him up.

Getting underneath him and getting him to his feet was a battle. We both fell several times, and I was pretty sure I bruised my tailbone. But we finally got him standing. Then we had to fight our way up the steep, slick hill through severe wind and rain. I could see why Jake had fallen with two good legs; it was hard staying upright, and even harder supporting someone. But together, we managed to get through it. By the time we both made it back to the bunker, we were sodden, freezing, sore, and in pain. I helped him sit down at the table and prop his injured leg on a chair, and then I grabbed a blanket from a shelf and wrapped it around his shoulders.

After wrapping myself with another blanket, I squatted down by his leg to take a look at his ankle. He cringed the entire time I took his shoe off, and I cringed when I finally saw his ankle—it was really swollen. This was going to put him out of commission for a while.

"How is it?" he asked, face contorted in pain as he tried to sneak a peek at his injury.

"It's . . . not good," I told him. "You're going to need to stay off it for a while." And we'd both have to hope that it was just a sprain. Once again, it reminded me just how vulnerable we were out here. We might have found an unbelievable shelter full of much-needed supplies, but we didn't exactly have access to a doctor. We both needed to be very careful.

Jake sighed as he leaned back in the chair. "I don't have time to stay off it for a while."

I raised an eyebrow at that. Ever since we'd moved over here to the bunker, life had been easier for us. I didn't even need to fish every day. "I can handle the extra workload. I'll light the bonfire and gather water and wood. It will be fine."

Jake pursed his lips but nodded. "We should . . . probably talk about the fact that we kissed . . . again."

God, no, I didn't want to talk about it. Didn't want to tell him it was a mistake, didn't want to hear him apologize for being more than just friends with me. Not when my lips were still burning with the taste of him.

Wishing I had ice for his ankle, I poured some cold water from a canteen onto a towel. "I don't really think there's anything to talk about. Yes, it happened again, but my sister loves you . . . and you . . . you love her too. When we get back home, the two of you will be together again, so that kiss . . . it doesn't matter, so why talk about it?"

Jake let out a weary sigh, and as I moved away from him to sit on a chair nearby, he quietly said, "I care about Kylie . . . a lot. And there are times when that feels exactly like love, but . . . I don't know anymore, Valerie. Being out here with you . . . it's opened my eyes. Things are changing between us. Can't you feel that? Everything we were before, it's just . . . *more* now."

Pain, confusion, and gut-twisting guilt made me clamp my mouth shut and stare at the floor. We couldn't do this to my sister. "What about just being friends?" I whispered.

His voice was soft when he answered me. "I think a part of me will always care about Kylie, but I can't deny the fact that I care about you too. You mean so much to me, Valerie, and I just don't see the point in keeping ourselves apart anymore. Because let's face it: there's a real chance we're never getting off this island. In fact, I'd say the odds of us staying here are about a thousand times greater than the odds of us ever leaving."

The pain in his voice made me look up at him. I was so used to him being the positive one that it was jarring to hear him talk like that. I wanted to argue, wanted to keep the hope alive . . . but that wasn't how I really felt. "Yeah, I know," I muttered, feeling devastation settle around me. We were most likely going to die on this island, just the two of us, alone until the end of our days. So did it really matter if we betrayed my sister? We were probably never going to see her again.

He gave me a small smile as he shook his head. "So you see, that kiss *does* matter. It's just about the *only* thing that matters now."

A soft sigh escaped me as I gazed at his glorious face. "Yes, you're right; things *are* changing between us. You mean so much more to me now . . . and that terrifies me." My heart was already too invested in him. He could devastate me in an instant if he changed his mind. Or if we *did* ever leave this island. He was the one with the injury, but I was the one who felt vulnerable.

Jake's face turned solemn, like he perfectly understood what I was saying. "Would you believe me if I said it terrifies me too?"

I stewed on that for a while, then nodded. I supposed it was just as scary for him to not only admit to having feelings for someone else while still caring about his lost girlfriend but also to start the process of acting on those feelings—of saying it was okay for us to be together. God, what a messed-up situation we were in.

"You should lie down and rest," I told him, wanting to end the painful conversation.

"Will you lie down with me?" he asked, his voice surprisingly timid.

I frowned, and he held his hands up. "Just to rest, I swear. I just . . . want to be near you."

I sighed but nodded. How could I turn down a fantasy? I helped him hobble his way to the bed, then helped him sit down and prop his leg up on a stack of blankets. He patted the empty space beside him, and I timidly sat down. The change between us had been sudden and yet a long time coming—if such a thing was possible. But the months in isolation, with no real hope of reprieve, had escalated our natural feelings. I wondered if my sister would understand if she knew, or if she'd hate us. Maybe both.

I had trouble sleeping that night. My mind twisted and turned, mulling over the things that had happened between Jake and me—the kiss we'd shared and both of us admitting the horrible odds of ever getting off the island. Most likely, we were never leaving this tropical paradise, but . . . even if we somehow did, things would never be the same. Too much was different. I cared for Jake—always had—and he was open to returning those feelings. I should be elated, but all I felt was guilty. I was betraying Kylie. Although if I was going to be a realist, Kylie believed Jake was dead, and she was currently letting him go in her heart. She was releasing him, and I was picking up the pieces. It didn't feel quite so deceitful in those terms, but deep down I knew I was just trying to convince myself that what we were doing was okay.

With a sigh, I gave up on the sleep that wasn't happening and carefully crawled out of bed. Jake stirred a little as I left his side, a hand subconsciously reaching out for me. Soft smile on my lips, I bent down and kissed his fingers. It felt weird to do so—I'd been subduing my feelings for a really long time—but it felt wonderful, too, like it was meant to be.

My heart was overflowing with mixed emotions as I slipped on my shoes. I was so happy that things were escalating with Jake—he was the only man who'd ever truly stirred my soul. But at the same time, guilt weighed heavy around my heart. I loved Kylie and would rather chop off my arm than hurt her—so why was I pushing against the boundaries with her man? Trying to cross that line that should never be crossed? She wasn't even here, and I felt the weight of her eyes on me all the time.

How could you, Valerie? I trusted you.

I'm sorry, Kylie. I've loved him for as long as I've known him . . . same as you.

Rolling my eyes at myself, I pushed against the thick door to the bunker. It stuck a little, like something was blocking it. Fear shot up my spine. Oh my God, what if the storm had knocked down a handful of trees against the door, blocking our path? What if our only exit was sealed? Then we wouldn't be in a bunker . . . we'd be in a tomb.

Just as panic began to make my heart surge, the door popped open enough for me to get out. A long, relieved exhale left my lips as I stepped outside. Thank God, we weren't trapped, weren't doomed to starve to death. It had given me such a fright, though; my eyes started stinging, and my breath was still fast. As I put a hand on my chest to calm myself, I took a look around. Our little jungle was almost unrecognizable. Trees were broken, uprooted, or just completely gone. It was like a giant had come through with a broom, laying havoc on the land. That was way more than just a tropical storm, more like a hurricane.

If we hadn't found the bunker . . . if I'd left Jake outside to fend for himself . . .

I couldn't even contemplate either one of those scenarios.

Not knowing what else to do, I cleared the debris away from the bunker door. There were two felled trees in front of it, the top of one making it difficult to open the door. Another couple of feet to the left, and I wouldn't have been able to open it at all. That made our sanctuary suddenly feel like a potential prison. I'd have to fight through panic whenever a storm hit from here on out—I could tell already.

Pushing that worry aside for another day, I began working my way toward the bonfire beach. It was a mess when I got there. There wasn't even a hint of where our original bonfire had been. It would have to be completely rebuilt. As I stared at the sandy stretch of land, I debated whether we should keep trying to reach the outside world. They believed we were dead. They weren't looking for us. They'd already moved on. Shouldn't we?

But even as I thought that, I knew we couldn't stay here. Well, we couldn't stay here without trying to leave. Every day, we needed to at least try. The day that we truly accepted there was no hope was the day we'd begin dying inside; I was sure of it. The bonfire, no matter how trivial a thing it was, was actually providing us with our only source of hope. We couldn't abandon it. No matter how hard it was, we had to keep the hope alive.

That realization made me push forward. Made me gather every scrap of wood I could find. It was all wet and would never light, but I gathered it into a pile anyway. Tomorrow it might be dry enough. Or the day after, or the day after. The when didn't really matter; it was the act of doing it that was important. I wouldn't let us give up. We *would* get off this island. And then . . . well, we'd deal with that part once we got there.

Chapter Thirteen

For the next few days, I went out and lit the bonfire while Jake rested. He hated it. He wanted to be doing something more substantial than just lying down, but as I kept reminding him, it was necessary. The longer he rested, the quicker he'd heal.

On the morning of the fourth day, Jake had finally had enough of being benched. "The first day or two, I agreed with you, but now . . . I'm fine, Valerie." Standing from the bed, he gingerly put weight on his ankle. He managed to stand upright, but he couldn't hide his cringe.

I shook my head as I studied him. "Nope, it clearly still hurts, so you're still resting."

With a sigh, he crossed his arms over his chest. "It's fine, and I'm coming with you."

I wanted to object again, but I could tell from the look on his face that I wouldn't win the argument this time. Jake was either coming with me now or trailing after me once I left. Since it seemed safer to be beside him, I grudgingly agreed. "All right, all right, you can come."

He grinned, and it was so adorable I just wanted to loop my arms around his neck and spend the next fifteen minutes kissing him. But we weren't there yet. Actually, we hadn't kissed again since the storm, and the fact that we hadn't was kind of killing me. One taste wasn't enough.

"But don't you do something stupid and hurt yourself again. I don't need you permanently out of commission." A horrible image of Jake bloody and battered came to mind, and I bit my lip as fear tightened my stomach.

"Hey," Jake said, stepping toward me. "I'm fine. Everything is fine."

He cupped my cheek as he stood before me, and the icy panic instantly subsided. Staring into his jade eyes, I felt my heart begin to race. "You didn't limp," I told him, smiling.

"I told you I was fine," he said, grinning.

His thumb started caressing my cheek, and his eyes darted between mine. I could feel desire welling in me—an absolute need to press my lips to his. The guilt was nearly overwhelming, but I forcefully pushed it aside and allowed my feelings to sweep me away as I leaned up to kiss him. He immediately returned the intimate movement, and I wrapped my arms around him as I pulled him in deeper. My breath quickened as our kiss intensified. So did Jake's. His hand on my cheek shifted to my neck, then my shoulder, and he ran both hands around my body, pulling me in tighter. He wanted this just as much as I did.

When we finally separated, his eyes were blazing with need. I had to imagine mine looked the same. "Jake . . . ," I murmured, wondering what I could possibly say after a kiss like that.

Jake frowned as he studied my face. "Was that . . . too much?"

His question made me smirk. "You realize I started that, right?"

His face relaxed into a grin, and he laughed. "Yeah, I know, but . . . I just want to make sure . . ." The seriousness returned as his eyes bored into mine. "I want to make sure you're okay with this."

"I am," I said, bringing my hand up to cup his cheek. "To be completely honest, I've been wanting this for a long time. Wanting you for a long time. But I love my sister, and she . . ." Guilt and pain swelled inside me, and dropping my hand from his face, I looked away from him. "This is so hard. I want her to be happy, and you make her happy, but *I* want you too. Always have. And that made it really hard to be around you."

He briefly touched my chin, bringing my gaze back to him. "I'm sorry. I know I didn't help with that, but I'll be honest—being around you was hard for me too. When I was with Kylie, things were so good, it seemed like it was meant to be, but then . . . I'd see you, and all of a sudden, I wasn't as sure. Down was up. Up was down. It was . . . confusing. But I never meant to hurt you. I never meant to hurt anyone."

Our eyes locked, and I found I couldn't turn away from his gaze. Finally, after a few moments of silence, we both leaned toward each other, again seeking each other's lips and comfort. As our mouths melded together, an emotion built inside me—one I didn't want to ignore anymore. Love. I was so in love with this man. I poured my feelings into my kiss, letting him know what was in my heart, since I couldn't say the words.

Clutching his hands in mine, I began pulling us toward the bed. Jake broke away from our intense kiss when he realized where I was leading him. Heat was in his eyes as he glanced to the mattress, then back to my face. "Are you sure?" he whispered.

Touched that he was always looking out for me, I nodded. "I am if you are."

His mouth drifted back to mine. "I'm . . . yeah . . . I am."

Once his mind was made up, things between us intensified quickly. He pulled at my clothes while I pulled at his. Shirts fell to the floor, followed quickly by pants, then underwear. When we were both bare, he pulled us onto the bed. His mouth shifted to my neck while his hands drifted along my body. I was so ready for him, for us, that everywhere he touched me felt electric. When his finger swept between my legs, I cried out and clutched him closer. Needing him, needing more, I pulled him on top of me. He groaned as he sank inside me. I held my breath as I was hit with multiple overwhelming sensations. I'd wanted this for so long. *God, yes.*

Jake paused, breathing heavily against my neck. I turned my head to find his lips. I needed to feel as connected to him as possible right now. He kissed me eagerly, hungrily, and then he began to move inside me. A low moan escaped me as he stroked against all the right places. I'd never been with someone before who'd felt so . . . perfect. I could feel the need to release rising in me with each thrust of his hips, and I knew this wouldn't be nearly as long as I wanted it to be. But that was okay, because we had all the time in the world to do this now.

I didn't hold back, didn't try to stretch out the moment. It was coming, and I let it hit me. The wave of euphoria made my entire body tense up, stiffen. I cried out with joy as it swept me under. Then I felt Jake release, heard him curse under his breath and mutter something into my skin. Knowing he was experiencing this, too, intensified the moment. I felt like it would never end—I never wanted it to end.

But eventually the energy left our bodies, and we lay there, trying to collect our breaths and slow our hearts. I wasn't sure if it was because I'd wanted him for so long and he'd always been unobtainable, but I'd never felt anything as intense as that. Never felt so completely satisfied. And yet as happy as I was, I still ached for him, still longed to do that again.

Jake gave me a soft kiss, then rolled onto his back. I hated his absence and draped my arm over his stomach. We'd fallen into that so rapidly that I hadn't had a chance to explore his picture-perfect body. That was something I'd have to rectify soon.

I turned my head to look at him. He was smiling, his eyes closed. He looked so at peace; I hoped that was genuine. Peeking an eye open, he shifted to look at me. "How do you feel?" he asked, concern on his face.

"Relaxed, amazed . . ." *Completely in love with you.* "What about you?" I bit my lip as he sat up on an elbow, worried he'd feel differently about it than I did. But his smile only grew as he stared at me.

Reaching out, he grabbed a lock of my hair and twirled it in his fingers. "The same," he said.

"No regrets?" I asked, cringing.

He studied my face for a moment, and nerves battered my stomach. "I really thought I would feel . . . guilty or sad, but . . . I don't." He leaned over and placed his lips against mine. "Being with you just feels too right," he murmured against my skin.

"I know what you mean," I said, closing my eyes and enjoying the feel of him.

His lips shifted to my cheek, then my neck. "All I am right now is . . . happy."

The sudden nerves instantly transformed, shifting from anxiety to need. "Me too. But we should probably go light that fire . . ."

"I think I hear rain," he murmured, his lips trailing across my chest.

I sucked in a breath as his tongue swirled around my nipple. "Really?" I exhaled.

"Oh yeah," he said, his mouth closing around my nipple. "Sounds like a terrible storm . . . might last all day. We should stay inside." His lips left my chest and began making their way down my stomach. My breath quickened with every inch he went lower.

"Yeah, storm . . . we should definitely . . . stay inside." His tongue swept between my legs, and the ability to form words failed me. Yes, there was nowhere else I wanted to be right now.

~

We stayed inside the bunker all that day and all the next day, exploring every inch of each other over and over again. I was bleary eyed and a little wobbly when we finally got dressed and set off to do our chores, but I'd never felt so completely satisfied. I could definitely get used to this.

Even though it had been a while since I'd brought home fresh fish, I decided to go with Jake to light the bonfire. He was walking around well and seemed completely healed, but I still worried. All it would take was one wrong move out here, one misstep, and we'd have serious problems. That was a major reason why we lit the bonfire. As nice as it could be sometimes, we couldn't live on the island forever. Whether through hunger, disease, or an accident, the odds of us dying prematurely here were far too great.

Ax in hand, I followed Jake onto the bonfire beach. The stretch of ocean in front of us was overwhelming in scope. It was the only thing visible, and staring at it made it seem like the rest of the world was gone, replaced by an endless blanket of blue. I'd always enjoyed the water before, but right now, it just felt . . . lonely. Turning away, I helped Jake gather wood for the fire.

It took a while to cut logs and branches and drag them down to the makeshift firepit. It was hard work, and by the time we had the fire lit and crisply burning, Jake and I were both covered in sweat.

Wiping my face, I grimaced at him. "Want to go take a bath?" I said.

Jake gave me a playful grin, one I was beginning to know really well. "What's wrong with a little sweat?" he asked, pulling me into his body.

I cringed and laughed as our wet bodies collided. As the scent of a roaring fire filled my nose, Jake lowered his mouth to mine. We were dirty and gross, but I suddenly didn't care. I was reveling in the fact that he could be mine, nearly whenever I wanted him.

Feeling joyous, I pulled on his arms as I sat on the sand. He laughed as he came with me, then laid me back on the beach and resumed kissing me. I'd never made love out in the open before—never even considered it before—because nowhere back home was completely devoid of people. But here . . . there was literally no one around for miles. We could completely and freely be ourselves.

I started pulling at his clothes, hoping he'd be on the same page as me. As he stripped off his shirt, it was clear that he was. I ran my fingers down his taut abs, appreciating every line, tracing that wonderful tattoo.

Specks of sand drifted from my hands to his chest. We were going to have sand everywhere after this, but it would be totally worth it.

Jake brought his mouth to my neck. He kissed me a couple of times, sending lightning bolts down my body, then murmured, "Salty," in my ear.

With a laugh, I let my head fall to the side so I was looking out at the ocean. The vast nothingness was a comfort now, since it confirmed that no one would see what we were about to do. Only . . . it was no longer a tranquil sea of nothing. There was something out there, and it was coming closer.

I jerked upright to a seated position, almost smacking Jake in the head in the process. "What?" he asked, sitting beside me.

"There's something . . ." Narrowing my eyes, I stared out over the shimmering water, trying to understand what I was seeing. It had to be an illusion, because it sure looked like . . .

"Oh my God, a ship," Jake said, jumping to his feet as he confirmed my suspicions.

My heart started pounding in my chest as hope and adrenaline surged through me. Jake began waving his arms over his head, yelling at the top of his voice. I did the same. Desperation started overwhelming me. They had to see us, had to see our signal. They were so close . . . if they shot right by us, it would be soul crushing.

I screamed and waved until my throat was raw and my arms were too tired to lift. As I panted, trying to restore my energy, I saw a smaller boat on the water. This one was heading right for us. Tears leaked down my cheeks as relief flooded through me. They'd seen us. They were coming. We were going home.

Jake saw the rescue boat too. He turned to me with shimmering eyes. "We did it, Valerie. We made it."

We'd done it; we'd made it. All of this was over. But . . . not all of this had been bad. A flicker of fear dashed my joy as I watched Jake grab his shirt and slide it over his body. Our last intimate moment flashed through my mind. Was that the last time I'd ever hold him, kiss him . . . make love to him? Were we over, now that we were going back home . . . to my sister?

Not wanting to comprehend the magnitude of that potential loss, I grabbed his hand and squeezed. He clasped me back just as fiercely, then swept me into a hug. His body was vibrating with emotion, but I wasn't entirely sure what emotion he was feeling. Happiness to be leaving, sure, but happiness to be returning to Kylie, or sadness that the inner fire we'd been building had just been quenched? Maybe both. I knew I felt like sobbing and laughing.

It felt like it took forever for the small boat to inch up to the shore. Jake and I sat on the beach as we waited. Holding his hand, I rested my head against his shoulder and silently prayed that somehow this wasn't over between us. I wasn't sure how I could go on without him. Not after I'd allowed myself to fall completely in love with him. But I couldn't be with him either. I couldn't do that to Kylie.

The men on the rescue boat didn't speak English, but their faces were sympathetic as they handed us water and blankets, so I knew they understood our situation. They urged us onto the small boat, then pushed the boat into the water . . . and then we were gone, forever sailing away from the place that had changed our relationship. I watched the island get smaller in my vision with mixed feelings. Surprisingly, sadness was the most prevalent one.

Jake squeezed my hand, and I looked over at him. He had the same melancholy smile on his face, like he was going to miss it too. That made me feel a little better. At least I wasn't alone with these odd, conflicting feelings.

The small boat reached the larger boat, and we were hoisted up. Once we were on the deck, I looked back at the island. It seemed so tiny now, with only a trail of dark smoke to indicate it was even there. I suddenly wished we'd had a chance to collect some of our things—bowls Jake had made, shells I'd collected—but none of that stuff was truly important, and most of the things on the island hadn't been ours anyway. We'd just been allowed to borrow them for a time, and I would be eternally grateful for that.

A lot of the crew didn't speak English, so at first we didn't have a way to explain what had happened to us. It took a few minutes, but eventually they found a man who could speak our language. We brokenly told him our story, and he let us know where the boat was headed—Los Angeles. We were indeed going home. After all this time, it felt a little surreal.

Jake hugged me tight when we were on our way, and I clung to him with an almost maniacal desperation. I wanted to talk to him about us, about what we were now, but my throat was too tight for words, and my heart was too fragile. I couldn't handle having that conversation yet, so I didn't say anything.

Chapter Fourteen

I was a nervous wreck on the ride back home. Both because I was trapped on a boat in the middle of the ocean again and because I wasn't sure what to expect when we finally arrived back home. Jake and I talked about a lot of things during the journey, but not about us. He tried to open the conversation a few times, but I didn't let him. I wasn't ready to say goodbye, and I was certain that was what was going to happen. Kylie loved him, and since it had only been a few months, there was no way she'd given her heart to someone new. She needed him, and I wasn't about to stand in the way of her happiness.

I never would have let anything happen between Jake and me in the first place if I'd known we'd be rescued. Both of us had convinced ourselves that this day would most likely never happen, but now it was here. We were back in LA.

Jake stepped up to my side as I watched the pier getting larger and larger. "Surreal, isn't it?" he said, taking in the hustle and bustle of the city we could see around the waterline. "It all seems so crowded after the jungle. Noisy."

I smiled up at him, then leaned into his side. "Yeah. I always thought there was nowhere on earth I could live other than LA, but now . . . now I'm not so sure."

He nodded as he wrapped his arm around my shoulder. "Yeah, I'm gonna miss the quiet."

Closing my eyes, I enjoyed his embrace. Was this the last time I'd feel it?

"Valerie?" Jake softly said, squeezing my shoulder. "We should—"

Shaking my head, I slightly pulled away from him. "No, we shouldn't."

Jake sighed, then turned me to face him. "You can't keep running from this. We're almost home."

"I'm not running, Jake. I've already faced this, and I'm fine."

"You're fine. And what exactly are you fine with?" he asked, lifting an eyebrow.

Ice poured through my veins. I did *not* want to talk about this. I didn't want to acknowledge the fact that this was over. That *we* were over. "Going home . . . going back to our old lives."

"Going back to our . . . ? Valerie," he said with a sigh. "I don't even know what—"

"Jake," I said, stepping away from him. "I'm fine, and I don't want to talk about this. Let's just be happy we're back and not worry about . . . anything else. Okay?"

The look on his face was forlorn, sad, but he nodded and gave me space to process. We didn't say anything more to each other while the boat docked, and I felt the wall of tension between us. It was like a burr under my skin, foreign, irritating, and unescapable. I hated it, but it was what it was, and there was nothing I could do to change it.

When it was finally time to go, I hugged all of the crew, and even though most of them couldn't understand me, I thanked them for picking us up. It would have been a simple thing for them to ignore our call for help, and I would be forever grateful that they hadn't.

Jake followed me down the gangplank. I found myself continuously wanting to wait for him, hold his hand, but it was time to return to the real world, and in the real world, we weren't together. And not holding his hand turned out to be a good thing, because an unexpected sight greeted us—a crowd of people and reporters, including my mom and dad, all my friends . . . and my sister.

Someone on the boat had clearly contacted the authorities, let them know they'd picked up a couple of strays. I was so shocked to see people I knew that I was frozen in place. My sister's eyes locked on mine. Hers were red, like she'd been sobbing recently. She started crying again as I stood there staring at her. Then her eyes flicked past me to Jake. I couldn't turn, couldn't look at his reaction. All I knew was that he'd stopped when I had stopped. Was he silently supporting me . . . or was he just as stunned as I was?

I snapped out of it when I noticed my parents step up beside my sister. Mom was crying; Dad was rubbing at his eyes. Seeing them so emotional—seeing them at *all*—made hot tears prick my eyes. I'd missed them, of course, but it wasn't until this very moment that I realized just how much. I swallowed back the sob building in my throat, and then I rushed forward to meet my family and wrapped my arms around all three of them in an awkward group hug.

"Valerie, oh my God, we thought you were dead," my mom was saying. Kylie was sobbing incoherently, unable to form any words, and my dad was trying to keep it together. And failing.

As Mom kept repeating that she'd thought I was dead, I heard Jake next to us, greeting his own family. Kylie gave me one last squeeze, then tore away from me to go to him. I didn't want to watch their reunion, but it was impossible to ignore them.

Still sobbing, my sister jumped into Jake's arms, almost knocking him over. She wrapped her arms and legs around him, clinging to him with every inch of herself. I watched as Jake closed his eyes, squeezed her, and let out a long exhale. A smile formed on his face, and he looked genuinely at peace—like he could finally breathe again. It tore me open, and I half expected the ground around me to be covered in my blood.

Jake slowly opened his eyes, and our gazes locked. His expression shifted to one of pain and uncertainty. His mouth opened, and knowing an apology was about to come out of it, I quickly turned around to greet my friends. Jake had nothing to apologize for—as much as it hurt, he belonged with Kylie.

Alicia and Chloe both grabbed me at once; they were sobbing as they hugged me. Stephanie looked like she'd been crying, too, but while she waited her turn to hug me, her gaze shifted to Jake and Kylie. When she returned her eyes to mine, there was worry in them. She knew.

Bunching her brows, she mouthed, "Are you okay?"

The tears I'd been resisting poured down my cheeks. "No," I mouthed, shaking my head. Steph sighed, then moved Alicia and Chloe out of the way so she could comfort me.

"I'm so sorry," she whispered in my ear. Her words made me cry even harder, so much so that I was shaking in her arms. Steph pulled back, sympathy on her face. Then she gave me a sad smile. "I am really glad you're alive."

"Me too," I said, a chuckle escaping me.

Steph hugged me again, and then Alicia and Chloe joined her. As the three of them squeezed the life out of me, reporters tried to sneak through the crowd of people to ask Jake and me questions. "What happened to the boat? How did you survive? What happened on the island?" Not wanting to answer any of those things right now, I kept my mouth shut. So did Jake.

"Leave them alone. They've been through enough," my dad barked, pushing the shoulder of a particularly aggressive reporter.

Shielding me from the press, my mom started leading me to their car. "She'll talk to you when she's recovered from this shock. Now, if you'll excuse us, we need to get both of them checked out at a hospital. They have to be malnourished, exhausted . . . half near death."

The reporters let us walk away, and I shot a glance at Jake as he followed behind us, walking hand in hand with my sister. Physically,

Jake and I were far better than anyone would probably believe—thanks to the bunker and its ample food rations—but emotionally . . . yes, I was wiped.

Jake and I were separated at the hospital. My friends and my parents wouldn't leave my side; Kylie wouldn't leave his. The entire time the nurse checked my vitals, I imagined Jake and Kylie kissing. Voraciously. It made me sick to my stomach.

"I just can't believe you're alive," my mom murmured, stroking my hair. "We thought for sure . . . we had a funeral for you. And for Jake. Your sister . . . she's been doubly devastated."

Guilt tore through me at what Kylie had gone through. What she had to be going through now. What she *would* go through if she only knew what had really happened on the island. "I'm sorry," I whispered, not sure who I was talking to.

My mom let out a single sad laugh. "You're sorry? For what? You didn't do anything wrong. All you did was survive," she added, wrapping her arms around me in a hug.

Right. If she only knew what had happened with Jake, she might think differently about the situation. Or maybe not. Maybe she'd understand; maybe she'd forgive me. I could almost hear her saying, *It's fine, sweetheart. Just don't let it happen again. Jake belongs to Kylie.*

But was that still true? It had been months. Kylie had completely believed he was dead. They'd had a funeral. Maybe she'd met someone else. Maybe she'd fallen in love again. It was a little soon for that but not completely out of the question. I wasn't sure how to bring it up, but since I was genuinely concerned about my sister, I quietly asked, "How is Kylie? I mean . . . I saw how she is now, but how was she before she knew we were alive? How was she a few days ago?"

Mom bunched her brows, like she wasn't sure what I was asking. Then she sighed. "We've been really worried about her, actually. She never really . . . accepted that you and Jake were gone. She's been clinging to the past, drowning in her pain, and not . . . moving forward."

She smiled. "But I'm sure she's going to be fine now. You're back, Jake's back . . . everything is perfect again."

Clinging to the past? Drowning in her pain? Not moving forward? Every word Mom said was a dagger to my heart—she'd gone through so much. But Mom's comment about things being perfect now? Hardly. Because as relieved as I was that Kylie would be getting better now, I couldn't stop feeling Jake's hands on my body, his mouth on mine. I'd gotten so used to it that it felt unnatural now to not hug him, hold him, kiss him. No, we couldn't *all* be happy in this situation. One of us—or maybe all of us—was going to be in misery.

The doctor gave me the all clear, and my parents took me home. With them. Because I no longer had a place of my own. Upon my death, my apartment had been given up, all my things given away or sold. I was starting life over again. At least I hadn't had too much to begin with.

The first thing I did when I got home was take the world's longest shower. It felt incredible to be really clean again. We'd had soap and shampoo thanks to the bunker, but a waterfall just wasn't a shower. When I got out, I saw that Mom had stacked a bunch of her clothes on the bed in my old bedroom. She'd even given me a pair of flip-flops to wear instead of my ancient military boots.

She knocked on the door once I was changed. "How was it?" she asked, a huge smile on her face.

"Absolutely amazing," I said, grinning. Sitting on the bed, I looked around the empty bedroom. Besides some furniture, the only things in here were some neutral pastel paintings on the wall. Everything I'd once had was gone. "Was all of Jake's stuff sold too?" I asked, looking up at her.

Mom shrugged. "Yeah. Kylie had a really hard time with that. She wouldn't let his parents get rid of anything for the longest time, but eventually . . . they did. I suppose he'll be staying with her now." She pursed her lips, like she wasn't sure how she felt about that. I knew how

I felt about it. Sick. He could be making love to her *right now. I thought you were dead, but you're not* sex—the ultimate makeup sex. I was going to throw up. But I shouldn't be sick. This was how things were supposed to be. Jake and Kylie in love and headed toward marriage. And me . . . trying to move forward without him.

After a dinner large enough for six people, Mom and Dad went to bed. I sat on the cold mattress, wondering how I would ever get to sleep. I'd gone to bed with Jake by my side for months now. Even on the boat, when we hadn't really been speaking, we'd cuddled at night. This would be the first time since the island that I'd truly slept alone. I hated it.

The hours ticked by, but still sleep evaded me. I tried everything. Lying still for an eternity, counting sheep, trying to completely clear my mind. But Jake was at the forefront of my brain, and nothing but him would fill this hole.

Maybe I should call him. Maybe his voice would be enough to ease my spinning mind. But neither one of us had cell phones at the moment, so I'd have to call my sister to talk to him, and that would be hard to explain. *Sorry, Kylie, I just can't sleep until Jake tucks me in.*

With an annoyed sigh, I looked over at the clock. God. It was just a few hours until morning. I was at the point where I might as well just stay awake, but I didn't want to stay awake. I wanted to fall asleep . . . with Jake by my side. And that was when I heard him.

"Valerie."

I sat up and walked over to the window, where I could hear his voice. Opening the curtains, I gaped as I saw Jake standing there, holding my window screen. "Oh, good, this *is* your room. I had a horrible vision of waking up your mom and dad."

After unlocking the window, I slid it open. "What are you doing here?" I asked, truly mystified.

Jake motioned inside. "Can I come in?"

I numbly nodded and stepped aside. Maybe I *had* fallen asleep and was dreaming. Yes, that had to be it. That was the only thing that made sense. Jake was supposed to be with Kylie right now, not crawling through my window. He slid it closed behind himself, then turned to face me. I was still gaping at him, stunned. "What are you doing here?" I asked again.

Jake cringed, then walked over to my bed. "I couldn't sleep. I think I got used to being next to you." Sitting on the bed, he looked up at me. "Did you know I'd never lived with a girl until you?"

Smiling softly, I sat next to him. "No, I didn't know that. I couldn't sleep either. It's so weird—I'm home, but I feel . . ."

"Homesick?" he said, grabbing my hand.

Blood rushed through my veins at the contact. I searched his face, wondering what he was really doing here. "Yeah," I whispered. "Homesick." Because somehow, in the relatively short amount of time we'd been together, he'd become my center, and now that he was gone, I was completely lost. My eyes welled as I stared at him. I missed him so much. How could I miss him this much when barely any time had passed? "You shouldn't be here," I said, swallowing the emotion threatening to clog my throat.

His fingers reached up and brushed my cheek. "Where else would I be?"

"With Kylie." A tear I couldn't hold back fell to my skin. Jake brushed it away.

He sighed, then looked down. "It's not that simple, Valerie."

"Yes, it is," I said, standing. "She's your girlfriend."

He shot off the bed to stand beside me. "Then why couldn't I stay with her tonight? Why did I tell her I needed to be with my parents tonight, needed to make sure they were okay? And then why did I come here instead?"

Tears filled my eyes as I stared at him. "I don't know. You're supposed to be with her. You wanted to come back for *her*, before it was too late, and you lost her. It's not too late. She's still crazy in love with you, and you . . . you love—"

He cut me off with a shake of his head. "No, I don't love her. I care about her, yes, absolutely." Stepping forward, he grabbed my hands. "But seeing her again made me realize . . . without a doubt . . . that I'm one hundred percent head over heels in love *with you.*"

I closed my eyes as his words washed over me. He was in love with me. I'd been waiting an eternity for him to say that, and now that he had . . . I was more confused than ever. Tears rolled down my cheeks as pain washed over me in waves.

Jake's fingers brushed the tears away. I could feel him, his face dangerously close to mine. "Valerie," he whispered. "I love you. Please say something."

Opening my eyes, I blinked away the moisture until I could clearly see him. He was gorgeous in the moonlight, his jade eyes deeper and more penetrating than ever. He wanted me. He was mine, if I'd just let him be mine. All I had to do to have him was betray someone I loved very much. *She'll never forgive me for this.* But it was *Jake.*

"I love you too," I whispered. The words warmed my heart, but saying them also made me feel like I'd been plunged into the ocean again and was drowning. "Jake, we'll destroy her. We should ignore this, leave it on the island." I felt like I'd dumped a vat of acid on my heart, and the feeble organ was screaming in pain. Leaving us behind was the right thing to do, but I really didn't want to do it.

Jake shrugged. "I can't, Valerie." He grabbed my hand and put it over his heart; I could feel it pounding under my fingertips. "How could I possibly leave *this* on the island? You're with me wherever I go. You always will be . . . and if I'm being perfectly honest with myself, you have been since the first day I met you." With a huge smile, he shook his head. "You like the same obscure anime, you make lasagna better than my Italian grandmother—something I never imagined was possible—and every so often, I hear you humming my favorite song. You're thoughtful, caring, empathetic, driven . . . beautiful. You're everything I've ever wanted in a woman. It's like you were made for me, Valerie, and I'm sick and tired of denying that."

As his words dazzled my mind, he brought his lips to mine, and the pain in my heart evaporated with our connection. He loved me, he wanted me . . . and I was far too weak to resist him.

I yanked off his shirt as I pulled him back toward the bed. He kicked off his shoes, then started undoing his jeans. God, was this really happening . . . here? Back at home? Once his jeans were off, he wrapped an arm around my waist and lowered us both to the bed. He lay on top of me, and I knew without a doubt—yes, this was happening.

As his fingers deftly removed my clothes, I tried to forget that what we were doing was wrong. It hadn't felt wrong on the island, and that hadn't been all that long ago. A couple of days, that was all. Forcing the negative feelings from my mind, I fixated only on the feel of him. The taste. God, he was a good kisser. I almost whimpered when his mouth left mine and began trailing down my neck. He sucked a nipple into his mouth, and I had to remind myself not to make a sound. We weren't alone anymore.

His mouth ran down my side, kissing along my obliques, then my hip. I was squirming with need, desperate for his touch, when he finally ran his fingers between my legs. I almost contained the moan, and he peeked up at my face to smile at me.

Grinning, I pushed him onto his back, returning the favor as I kissed my way down his chest. He shivered when my tongue began to outline his tattoo, then clutched the sheets and squirmed. I knew if we hadn't been within earshot of my parents, he'd have groaned. Loudly.

Continuing onward, I kissed his hip while clutching his hard body in my hand. I slowly, teasingly ran my tongue over the tip of him. He let out a soft curse, one he couldn't contain. The sound brought back every memory I had of making love to him. Not able to stand any more teasing, I shifted my hips on top of his, positioned him, and then pushed him inside of me. His head dropped back as his hand shifted to clench my hip. I wanted to cry out so badly; it was agony not to make a sound.

I slowly began to move, craving and savoring the perfect feeling of his body. Before long, the languid movements became more frantic, more urgent, and I dropped my chest to his so I could kiss him. "I love you," he whispered between my lips.

I wanted to repeat the sentiment, wanted to scream to the world that I felt the same, but the moment of release was upon me, and all I could do was gasp as euphoria hit me like a brick wall. Jake grabbed both of my hips, urging me on, then stiffened, biting his lip as a quiet groan escaped him. Our pace slowed, then stopped, and our breaths eventually returned to normal. But still, we lay there, connected, like we were both afraid to move, both afraid to acknowledge what we'd done.

This wasn't our first time together, but somehow . . . this changed everything.

Chapter Fifteen

Pale light began to seep through my window, and I knew my early-rising parents would be awake soon. I didn't want Jake to leave, but I knew he had to go. Mom and Dad couldn't walk in here and find him in bed with me. They wouldn't understand. I barely did.

We'd made love again. Here, back at home, away from the island. He'd admitted that he was in love with me. I loved him, too, but . . . Kylie. Mom had said she'd barely survived Jake's death. If Jake and I did this—committed to being a legitimate couple—it would almost be worse than us dying, for Kylie. Her relationship with Jake would end, but Jake would still be around the city, a ghostly reminder of what they'd once shared. She would lose him again, and she would lose me, too . . . since I strongly doubted she would ever want to see me again if I stole her boyfriend. I loved Jake with all my heart, but how could I do that to her?

A problem for another time. Right now, I needed to get Jake out of here.

"Jake, you should go," I murmured, poking his shoulder.

He let out a rumbling sound of contentment. "Can't. Too comfy."

I pushed his shoulder harder. "You need to, Jake. My parents can't find you here."

Opening his eyes, he looked over at me. "Yeah . . . okay. Guess I'll head back to my parents' place. It's so weird having everything I owned . . . gone." He shook his head. "It's weird to be starting over. No job, no place, no . . ." He let that trail off, but I understood what he'd been thinking. No girlfriend. But that wasn't true. He had me.

Giving him an encouraging smile, I said, "I know how you feel, but you're not alone. Just like on the island . . . together is how we'll get through this."

He grinned at me, then frowned. "What about Kylie? We need to tell her . . . something."

I felt like he'd just placed a cement block on my chest. "I know. I just don't think now is the right time." Because how would she ever accept me dating her ex-boyfriend? Who she didn't yet realize *was* her ex-boyfriend?

He raised an eyebrow at me. "Do you want me to keep pretending things are fine between us? That I'm in love with her and I'm not daydreaming about her sister?"

His comment made me smile even as the weight on my chest grew heavier. "Not forever, just . . . for now. She's been through so much . . ." I couldn't crush her heart yet. I wasn't sure if I would ever be able to do that.

"Yeah, I know," he said with a sigh. "I feel like a horrible human being."

"You're no more horrible than I am."

He sighed again, then groaned and sat up. "Okay, I'm leaving." He started to stand but paused to look back at me. "No matter what happens from here on out, just remember that I love you."

His words were both sweet and sad. I could feel the tears prick my eyes, but I swallowed them back. "I love you too," I whispered.

He leaned down to kiss me, then got up, dressed, and left out my window. A long sigh escaped me as I replayed our night over and over. It had been amazing, as always, but I was left with so many questions.

What were we doing? What were we going to do next? And most importantly, what were we going to tell my sister? Was there any way out of this that didn't break someone's heart?

No. There wasn't.

I managed to fall asleep due to pure exhaustion, and when I woke back up, my room was bright with sunshine. Glancing at the clock, I saw that I'd slept far longer than I'd wanted to sleep—it was almost noon. I was a little surprised my parents had allowed the long slumber. They were notorious for waking my sister and me up at the crack of dawn; eight was sleeping in when I was a child. But I supposed it wasn't too surprising that they'd let me catch up on my rest. To them, I'd been sleeping on the cold, hard ground for months. When they found out how cushy I'd had it, I was sure the early wake-ups would begin again.

With a yawn, I stretched and got out of bed. That was when I remembered that I was naked. Because I'd spent a good portion of the night with Kylie's boyfriend. No, I needed to stop thinking of him that way. Things had irrevocably changed between us, and soon Kylie would know that . . . and their ties would be severed. And then *my* ties with my sister would be too. Just the thought made me feel sick with guilt and shame. Was love enough of a reason to lose her forever?

I hurriedly dressed. I really hoped neither of my parents had checked on me while I'd been sleeping. They might wonder about the lack of clothes. Not that they would say anything—I *was* an adult, after all, and if I wanted to sleep nude, I certainly could.

The doorbell rang just as I entered the living room. Not seeing Mom or Dad anywhere—they must have gone to work—I opened the door. The visitor surprised and delighted me. "Steph," I exclaimed, leaning over to hug her. She didn't return the hug; she was holding a large cup of coffee in each hand. "Oh my God . . . coffee."

She handed one my way, and I immediately took it from her. It was still superhot, but I took a sip anyway. It was sweet and creamy and absolute heaven going down. "Oh my God, I haven't had coffee in ages.

Sometimes on the island, I would have dreams about coffee shops." That had been one commodity that the bunker hadn't provided for us, and I'd been aching for it.

Steph laughed as she stepped into the house and closed the door. "I thought you might enjoy that. Now . . . do you want to tell me what happened on the island? What *really* happened?" She let out a ragged exhale. "How did you even survive, Val?"

I paused in drinking my coffee. Memories of the wreck flooded my mind. They were quickly replaced with images of Jake. Him running down the stairs to me. Him finding me in the water, kicking us to safety. Spotting the piece of decking. Him giving me hope when I'd lost all of mine.

"Jake," I whispered, feeling my eyes begin to burn with emotion. "He literally ran to my rescue. I only made it out of the boat because of him."

Steph sighed, sympathy on her face. "And then you were stranded on an island together. Alone with your sister's boyfriend, a man you've had a crush on since before you even knew they were together."

I winced, then looked around the room, just to make sure we were truly alone. "Would you believe me if I said that nothing happened?"

She pursed her lips and raised her eyebrows. "If you promised, yes, because you wouldn't lie to me . . . right?"

With a groan, I sat down on the couch. "Best friendship is sometimes really annoying."

She laughed as she sat beside me. "I know. Spill. You'll feel better."

Realizing that was true, I turned to face her. "At first it was just attraction."

She crinkled her nose. "Weren't you both sweaty and dirty?"

I laughed, then sighed. "It really didn't matter, Steph. There was something between us . . . we eventually kissed." I sighed again. "And then he apologized. Said he would do better at being a friend."

Steph took a sip of her coffee, then shook her head. "I bet that lasted long."

"Longer than you'd think. Almost three months long."

She choked on her coffee. "Three months? Jesus. No matter what else happened, I'm seriously proud of you guys. You obviously tried to be good."

I smiled at her comment, and I actually felt a little better. "Thank you." I frowned. "If we'd just held out a little longer, that might have been the end of it. But there was a storm . . . I thought I was going to lose him . . . we kissed again, but it was different that time. Passionate, desperate. We admitted that we cared about each other, and then . . . and then we made love. Several times."

Steph giggled, and I groaned and laid my head back on the couch. "I'm a horrible person."

With a shake of her head, she said, "No, you're not. I really think you could have taken him that night at the bar. You could have betrayed your sister way back then. But you didn't. You did nothing with the man you'd been obsessing over. And then the unthinkable happened, and he became your savior. But still you did nothing, nothing more than a couple of kisses. You waited three months to cave into your feelings, and by then you probably honestly felt like you were never leaving the island. In my eyes, you're pretty freaking innocent, Val."

Her words of encouragement lifted the lead around my heart and made a huge smile break over my lips. "Thank you. I actually really needed to hear that."

"You're welcome," she brightly said. "Lifting your spirits is just one of the many services I provide as a best friend."

I laughed, then sighed. "I hope Kylie sees it the way you do."

"You're going to tell her?" she asked, eyes wide with surprise.

The incredulous look on her face made me frown. Did she think Jake was going to go back to Kylie and pretend that the island had never happened? "Yeah, I mean, we kind of have to tell her. We want to be together. He . . . um, came by last night." A sheepish smile formed on my face as I thought of our magical night wrapped in each other's arms.

Steph's face fell as she looked at me. "Oh . . . oh, Valerie."

"What?" I asked, setting my coffee down. "I thought you were proud of me? I thought you supported this?"

"I was proud, I *am* proud, but I don't know . . . this is going to end *badly*." With a sigh, she put her coffee down as well. "I don't know if you've heard, but your sister was a wreck when she thought you had both died. I mean, we all were, but Kylie . . . she was really a mess. I didn't know if she was ever going to come out of it. Doing this to her . . . this is going to do some damage."

Hearing my own fears spoken out loud made guilt and shame flood through me. "What are we supposed to do? I love him, and he loves me. He can't ignore his feelings and stay with her because he's afraid to hurt her. She's going to lose him either way. Do I have to lose him too? After everything we've been through? Just to keep Kylie from a little more pain?"

Steph stared at me for a few moments before finally shrugging. "I honestly don't know. But . . . I think you're probably on the right track. No, you are on the right track. You're right. You can't keep things the same just to spare her pain. You'll just have to hurt her carefully," she finished with a cringe.

My eyes welled at the thought of breaking my sister's heart. "Great. Can't wait."

My parents came home right as Steph was leaving. I was surprised to see them since it was the middle of the afternoon. "Hey . . . what are you doing home?"

Mom laughed. "We live here, honey."

I rolled my eyes at her comment, then shook my head. "I meant, Why aren't you at work?"

Mom looked over at Dad before meeting my eyes again. "We, uh . . . we sold the business, and we're pretty much retired now."

Surprise hit me hard, but it dissipated quickly. They'd talked about this before, so it wasn't that big of a shock; I just hadn't expected it yet. "Oh, well . . . congratulations. I know you'd been wanting to do that for a while. I guess I truly am out of a job, though. Good thing I don't have any bills. Or anything, actually." I tried to smile, but it just wouldn't form.

Mom tossed her arms around me with a sigh. "I'm so sorry, Valerie. If we'd known there was even a possibility that you had survived, we wouldn't have . . ."

She sighed again, and I squeezed her. "It's fine, Mom. I'm not mad; it's just . . . weird."

Mom pulled back to look at me with a raised eyebrow. "My daughter came back from the dead. *Weird* just doesn't cut it."

With a laugh, I hugged her again. "You know I was never actually dead, right?"

Mom laughed, then patted my back. As Dad squeezed my arm, I let out a sigh. "Guess I should get a job. And my own place. And another car. And clothes. And a bed. And a toothbrush . . ." There were so many things I needed that it really was like I was back on the island. There was so much to do it was overwhelming.

"Don't stress," my dad said. "We're here to help."

I smiled at his offer, and I knew I would need them for some things, but neither one of them had an income now. I needed to do this on my own.

I was sifting through the help wanted ads on my mom's phone when another visitor arrived. This one was expected, although not at this time of day. "Hey, Kylie. Slow day at the beach?" Nerves began poking holes in my stomach as my sister sat down on the couch beside me.

Mom looked up from her book with a frown. “She doesn’t do that anymore.”

Kylie rolled her eyes at Mom while I said, “Oh, why not? You were so good at it.”

She shrugged, looking uncomfortable. “My heart just wasn’t in it.”

I could understand that. “So what do you do now?”

She started picking at a thread on her shirtsleeve. “I’ve been bouncing around, a little of this, a little of that.”

Mom’s eyes narrowed. “She’s had six jobs. Her longest one lasted three weeks.”

“Yeah, well, none of them were the right fit for me,” she countered, lifting her chin.

“None of them would let you get away with drinking on the job.” Her eyes grew more intense while mine widened in surprise. That didn’t sound like Kylie at all.

Kylie pursed her lips in annoyance. “That was *one* job, Mom. And I learned my lesson. No more day drinking. On workdays.”

She’d lost her job because she’d been drinking? My guilt compounded as I realized just how right Steph was about Kylie. She hadn’t just fallen apart—she’d broken apart. “Oh . . . Kylie . . .”

Kylie twisted her head to frown at me. “If you’re about to start in on a lecture, don’t worry about me. Yes, I went through a hard spell when you and Jake . . . but I’m better now.” Her lip trembled, and her eyes watered. “Jesus, Val, I thought you were dead, and I thought it was my fault. I’m the one who convinced you to go.”

I wrapped my arms around her in a hug, and she broke into tears. “I’m so sorry,” she said.

She was sorry? God . . . this was so much harder than I’d thought it would be. And I’d thought it was going to be hell. “It wasn’t your fault, Kylie. You couldn’t have known. Who would have ever imagined that happening?”

I felt miserable as I held her. And guilty. *I should tell her the truth about Jake and me. I should be honest about what happened on the island . . . and off the island.* But she was so broken that all I wanted to do was ease her pain and maybe get her help before I steamrolled over her heart—before she lost us again.

Pulling away from her, I put on a smile and changed the subject. "I thought you'd be at dinner last night. I missed you."

The redirect worked. She cringed. "Yeah, sorry. Jake wanted to spend time with his parents, and I wanted to be with him, so I had dinner over there. Please don't be mad."

I shook my head as pain washed through me. *You're the one who should be mad.* "It's fine. At least you're here now."

Kylie sighed as she sank back onto the couch. "Yeah . . . last night was kind of . . . weird."

Ice shot up my spine. "Weird? How?"

She tilted her head as she looked between Mom and me. "Jake was . . . off. Kind of distant . . . preoccupied. And he didn't want to stay at my place. That was so weird to me. I thought for sure he'd want to . . ." She let that trail off as she looked over at Mom.

"You thought he'd want to crawl all over you?" Mom said.

Kylie flushed with color and laughed a little. I felt a bit of nausea run through my entire body at the thought of her and Jake together. It quickly turned to remorse. Jake had been crawling all over *me* last night.

"Yeah, but maybe it's just too soon," she said, her eyes returning to me. "You guys did go through a lot. He told me how he saved you."

I swallowed a sudden lump in my throat. "It was awful . . . I've never been so scared." Not wanting her to dwell on my time with Jake on the island, I told her, "But we're fine now, and we're home. Everything is exactly how it's supposed to be." I squeezed her hand as I said it, knowing that while I was trying to be encouraging, I was also being incredibly misleading. Things might be how they were supposed to be, but they also weren't how they used to be. Kylie just didn't know that yet.

Mom was watching both of us with critical eyes, but then she smiled. "Valerie is right, honey. Jake just needs time to adjust to how things are now. We all do." Then her gaze shifted to just me, and I felt like she was telling me something. Whether she knew or suspected, I wasn't sure, but she was definitely warning me to not hurt my sister.

Chapter Sixteen

That night, I once again couldn't sleep. And it wasn't only because I'd gotten used to sleeping beside Jake and had trouble relaxing without him. Hanging out with my sister—knowing the things that I knew—had been difficult. Guilt and worry were swarming around me, and my heart was heavy with anxiety.

When it was just three or four hours before dawn, and I still couldn't sleep, I heard a familiar tapping on my window. Smiling, I hopped out of bed to see Jake standing there, goofy grin on his gorgeous face. I unlocked the window to let him in. Once he was all the way inside with the window closed, I tossed my arms around him. Our mouths met, and I poured my heart and soul into the kiss.

"I missed you," I murmured during a break.

"I missed you too," he answered.

The kiss grew heated, almost frantic. You would think we hadn't seen each other in years, not hours. Eventually, I pulled away from him. I was surprisingly breathless. His jade eyes were heated, his breath fast. He took a step toward me, like he wasn't done kissing me. I held up a finger, and he backed off. Then he let out a quiet laugh.

"Sorry . . . there's just something about you. I can't get enough."

I knew the feeling, but there was something we needed to talk about. Or rather, someone.

I sat on the bed with a sigh. "Kylie came over today."

Jake sat beside me with an equally grim sigh. "Yeah . . . she mentioned that she wanted to catch up with you."

A weird squirmy feeling washed through me at hearing him mention that he'd communicated with my sister. But of course he'd talked to her. They probably talked more often than Jake and I talked. In everyone's mind, including Kylie's, they were the couple. And Jake and I, we were just . . . well, I wasn't exactly sure what we were. I knew what I wanted us to be; I just didn't know how to get there.

"Kylie, she was hit hard by what happened to us. Really hard. Did you know that she stopped drawing caricatures at the beach?"

Jake's eyes widened, and he shook his head. "No," he whispered. "I didn't know that."

"Did you know she's been bouncing around from job to job, not happy anywhere?" Again, he shook his head. A soft sigh escaped me. "Did you know she was fired once because she was caught drinking on the job?"

Jake raised an eyebrow at that. "Kylie? Was drinking at work? She didn't mention that. Any of that."

"I can't imagine she's too proud of it." Disbelief flooded me as I shook my head. "It's so bizarre, isn't it? Not like Kylie at all . . . and that terrifies me."

He tilted his head as he studied me. "Terrifies you?"

I chewed on my lip before saying anything. "I'm worried about how she's going to handle our news. I'm worried she *won't* handle it. I'm worried she'll fall back into that despair that had her drinking at work. I'm just . . . I'm scared for her."

Jake sighed, then grabbed my hand. "Do you want me to go?" His voice was so soft I almost didn't hear his question.

Scrunching my brow, I shook my head. "No, I want you to stay. For a few hours at least." I gently put my hand against his cheek. "I don't want to end this. I just . . . I don't know what to do about her."

"Let's sleep on it," he said. "Maybe something will come to us." I lifted an eyebrow as he patted the bed. He grinned, then shook his head. "Just sleep, I swear."

Suddenly feeling exhausted, I crawled under the covers with him. Holding him tight, our arms and legs wrapped around each other, I felt completely and perfectly at peace. I really hated that something that made me feel so good, so alive, was also something that made me feel horrible.

Jake was gone when I woke up in the morning. I'd been so out of it I hadn't even heard him leave. He'd left a note on my pillow, though. It simply said, *I love you*. I clutched it to my chest and giggled like I'd never been in love before. And maybe I hadn't been. All of this felt really new. New, exciting, and guilt inducing.

After tucking the note under my pillow, I sat up on the bed and stretched. I'd really hoped I would open my eyes and be suddenly struck by some wondrous solution to our problem, but that hadn't happened. I still had no idea what to do.

~

Every night that week, Jake came in through my window and spent a few hours by my side. We didn't make love every time, but we always cuddled. And fell even deeper in love. We'd need to tell my sister soon. We couldn't keep meeting up behind her back, and Jake couldn't keep sneaking in through my window. One of these days, a neighbor was going to see and call the cops on him. Or even worse, my parents would hear him stumbling inside and walk in on us while we were together. *That* would be absolutely mortifying.

Smiling, content, and comfortable in bed with him, I nestled against his chest. "Jake, you know we can't keep doing this, right?"

He let out a satisfied noise. "Yeah . . . I know."

Biting my lip, I traced a circle on his bare chest. "Kylie must be curious why the two of you aren't . . . ?"

He turned his head to look at me; his eyes were more blue than green in the moonlight. "If you're asking me if I've been with her since we came back from the island, the answer is no. You're the only woman I've been with."

His admission made me grin. Then frown. "She has to be wondering why. It's been long enough that she has to know something is wrong."

His gaze drifted back to the ceiling. "Yeah . . . she wants to talk tonight. I don't know what to tell her."

Fear and ice filled me, but I pushed it back. We couldn't keep avoiding this. It wasn't making things better for Kylie. In fact, it was probably making things worse. "I think . . . you should tell her about us," I said. Then I sighed. "No. I'm her sister; *I* should be the one to tell her about us. I should have already."

Jake's arms around me tightened. "No . . . I'll do it." I twisted to look at him, and he let out a heavy sigh. "What happened between us, it doesn't change the fact that I fell out of love with her. Regardless of you and me, I need to talk to her simply because I don't feel the same way about her anymore. And that's something *I* should have told her already."

I nodded, then briefly closed my eyes. "This sucks."

"At least it will be over soon," he whispered.

I wasn't sure if he was right. This would forever alter things between Kylie and me. She was going to hate me after this. Could I handle that? I really wasn't sure. "I should go with you when you tell her."

Jake sighed and shook his head. "No. The minute she sees you, she'll know. I need to do this alone. It's the only way she doesn't . . ." He paused, then sighed again. "No, either way she'll be hurt, but at least this way I can ease her into it."

I nodded, then clenched him tight. I wasn't ready. I was also *overly* ready.

He inhaled a deep breath like he was steeling himself, and then he kissed my head. "I should go. Your parents will be up soon." We'd already had one close call, when he'd still been here after they'd woken up. I'd been terrified the entire time he'd snuck out the window, but my parents hadn't said a word about hearing anything strange. Thank God.

I missed him more than usual once he was gone. Probably because of what he was going to be doing later. It made me nauseous to think about it. The feeling only intensified as the day went on, and by the time evening rolled around—and I knew they had to be together—my stomach hurt so much it was cramping.

Sitting on the living room couch, I started biting my nails, an old nervous habit from when I was young. Mom noticed my mood and sat down beside me. "Everything all right?"

I tried to smile, tried to look like nothing was wrong, but I failed. Miserably. "I'll be fine, Mom. It's just . . ."

"You and Jake?" she asked, raising an eyebrow.

Dread numbed every nerve ending. What did she know? "What about Jake and me?"

She sighed, and then her eyes grew firm. I knew those eyes. Those were her *don't lie to me* eyes. "It doesn't take a genius to see that the two of you grew closer on the island. The question is . . . How close?"

That stare had made me admit to many things when I was younger. Surprisingly, maturity hadn't dulled its power. "We love each other. We want to be together."

She closed her eyes, then sighed. "I was afraid of that. I think Kylie probably is too." She opened her eyes; they were ringed with sadness. "Deep down, she has to suspect something happened between you two. Being alone for three months, thinking you'd never make it home . . . she has to be wondering; she's just too afraid to ask."

Feeling defeated, I sadly shook my head. "I fell in love with him, Mom. And he fell in love with me too. What are we supposed to do? Ignore that and lie to her?"

Mom shook her head. "I don't know . . . but I do know this will devastate her, Valerie, and she's been through *so* much. I hope you take that into consideration before you . . . do anything."

My eyes drifted to the ground as guilt and worry consumed me. *Too late, Mom. And I've been through a lot too.* I desperately didn't want to hurt my sister, but she had to know about us. I needed her to understand what had happened . . . and hopefully she would give us her blessing. Fat chance, though. She loved him too.

As I sat there, stewing, I wondered if Jake and Kylie were done . . . if they were over. Should I call his parents' house? See if he was home? We hadn't gotten cell phones yet. Or jobs. Jake was driving his dad's spare car, so he was doing slightly better than I was.

Wishing I could text him and ask him how things were going, I sat and waited. That was when a knock sounded on my parents' door. Mom was busy in the other room, so I answered the door for her. "Jake?" I looked behind him, but he was alone. He looked worn to the bone, and his eyes were red, like he'd been crying recently. "Are you okay?" I asked, my heart breaking at the sight of him.

"Can I come in?" he asked, his voice raspy.

"Yeah, of course." I opened the door wider, letting him come inside, then closed it behind him. He shuffled his way over to the couch and collapsed on the cushions.

Concern was shooting up my spine as I studied him. He was *not* okay. I'd known this was going to be hard on him, but I hadn't expected this reaction. I should have gone with him. We should have shouldered this pain together.

Sitting down on the couch beside him, I started rubbing his back. "Hey . . . how did it go? Was she furious?"

He stared ahead blankly, his expression so weary it was devoid of emotion. "She . . . she's never going to forgive you, Valerie. So long as you and I are together, she's going to hate you. And me." His dead eyes turned my way. "I'm fine with her hating me, but I can't handle splitting up a family. I can't handle her hating you for the rest of your life."

Pain squeezed my stomach while ice shot through my veins. "I'm sure she'll . . . someday, she has to . . ." I wanted to argue with him, but I knew he was right. I'd lost her. Tears filled my eyes, then spilled down my cheeks. "I should go talk to her. Tell her my side . . ."

Jake shook his head. "It won't matter. If we're together . . . it won't matter."

My brows furrowed as I stared at him. "What are you trying to tell me?"

Jake let out a deep sigh, then twisted to face me. He grabbed my hands, and I instantly felt like pulling them back. My heart started pounding as he stared at me. "She's basically making us choose. You and me or you and her."

I shook my head, and my throat tightened so much speech was nearly impossible. "There has to be another way."

His eyes watered as he stared at me. "There isn't. She's been through too much. She's . . . not the same, Valerie."

I closed my eyes, and more tears dropped onto my cheeks. "So I've lost my sister . . . she's gone forever." I could feel panic clawing at my insides, despair burning through my soul. I hadn't wanted to hurt her. I'd tried so hard, but I'd still failed.

Jake leaned over and gently kissed my cheek. "No. You won't lose your sister. It will take some time, but you'll get her back."

My eyes sprang open. "But you just said she'd never—"

He cut me off with the most painful words I'd ever heard. "We can't see each other again, Valerie. We have to end this so you can repair things with Kylie."

Fear and denial made me clamp onto his arms so tightly I knew I was bruising him. "No . . ."

The tears in his eyes fell down his cheeks. "I know. I don't want to either. But I can't live with destroying your family, and if you think about it . . . *really* think about it . . . I don't think you can either. The guilt, the pain . . . you'll end up hating yourself, and then you'll end up hating me. We'll break up anyway, only then it will be too late to save your sister."

"You don't know that," I whispered, but even as I said it . . . I knew he was right. Having Kylie torn out of my life would change me. It would change *us*. My head dropped as the truth settled over me.

"You see it now, don't you?" he softly said.

I released his arms and gently took his hands. "Yes." Just saying the word made something inside me die. Hope. The tenacious hold I'd had on hope for so long was finally dying. "Do we really have to do this?" I murmured, already knowing the answer.

He leaned his head against mine, and his voice hitched as he answered. "God, I wish we didn't have to . . . I love you so much, but yes . . . we can't be together." He pulled back to look at me with sorrowful eyes. "And . . . I think it has to be a complete break. No contact. Ever. I think that will make it . . . easier . . . in the end."

A sob escaped me, and I tossed my arms around him in a fierce hug. "I'll always love you, Jake. Always."

I felt him crying as he held me. "I'll always love you too. And every day we don't speak, just remember . . . I'm thinking about you. Even apart, we'll be doing this together."

The sobs came in earnest then. I couldn't believe this was actually happening, but he was right. It was the only way.

When our tears finally subsided, I felt like I'd aged a hundred years. Jake wiped my cheeks dry, a pained smile on his face. As I absorbed this last image of him, a tiny ember of hope flickered to life. "Maybe one day . . . when Kylie has forgiven me, when she's moved on . . . maybe then you and I can . . ."

I let the thought die, since it seemed improbable. It might take Kylie years to get over our betrayal, if she ever truly did. I couldn't exactly ask Jake to wait an endless amount of time for me, just sitting around hoping I'd eventually contact him. It would be cruel to even ask that.

Jake's smile grew even sadder. He knew the impossibility of what I was asking. "Yeah . . . maybe . . . one day." He sniffed, then looked around. "I should probably get going . . . lingering isn't going to make this any easier."

"Right," I said, feeling my chest tighten.

Jake sighed, started to get up, then twisted back to me. Before I knew what was happening, he was kissing me. It was painful, passionate, desperate. It was *don't forget me* mixed with *please move on with your life*. It tore me, but still, I didn't want it to end.

He pulled away suddenly, like he was forcing himself, and then he practically jumped off the couch and bolted to the door. He paused before opening it and looked back at me with watery eyes. "Goodbye, Valerie."

My lip quivered, and I begged myself not to start crying again. "Goodbye, Jake. I love you."

"I love you too," he whispered, and then he fled out the door. And out of my life.

Chapter Seventeen

I had a hard time sleeping that night. A part of me worried that Jake would show up, dashing our new resolve to pieces. Another part of me worried that he *wouldn't* show up, that we truly were over. I tossed and turned all night long until I finally woke up in the morning. I was alone, and I had been all night long. He hadn't come over, hadn't tried to mend us. We truly were finished. It was an agonizing realization, and if I was being honest with myself, it was one I wasn't prepared for. I spent the majority of the day sobbing in bed, a mere shadow of a person.

The next day I vowed to do better. And I did, only sobbing half the day. It took around three days without him for me to truly feel like I could begin to move forward . . . alone. And that was when the reporters started showing up on my parents' doorstep. Honestly, I was surprised they'd waited so long.

Dad tried to shoo them away, but I decided to speak to a few of them. It was actually pretty cathartic to talk about what had happened. I even talked about what had really happened with Jake and me—not in gory detail, but enough that it was obvious we'd fallen in love. Talking about him made me miss him. I hoped he missed me too. A tiny part of me hoped he always missed me, even though I knew it wasn't fair to wish that upon him.

"You really haven't talked to him?" Steph asked. We were at our favorite club, celebrating Alicia's birthday.

Sipping on my vodka cran, I shook my head. "No. Nothing since we decided to end things."

Steph pursed her lips as she absorbed that. "I understand why you guys broke things off, but . . . I can't help thinking maybe things aren't really over. Maybe there's still a chance for the two of you."

Pain pierced my calm, and I had to close my eyes to banish the hope she'd stirred. "Can we change the subject, please?"

"Sure," Steph said, empathy on her face. She shifted to look at Alicia. She was deep in a conversation with Chloe and hadn't been paying attention to us. "To the birthday girl," Steph said, holding out her drink.

Alicia immediately turned our way, a bright smile on her face. Chloe looked over with her, but her smile wasn't nearly so friendly. Chloe was good friends with my sister, and what I'd done to Kylie had blurred the lines of *our* friendship. Chloe only tolerated me now; Kylie still wasn't talking to me. I'd left a dozen messages, and all I'd received in return was silence from Kylie and glares from Chloe.

When we all clinked glasses, Chloe purposely avoided mine. It made me grit my teeth in annoyance, but there was nothing I could do about it. I couldn't exactly force Chloe to be my friend again. Or force my sister. Or forget about Jake . . .

God, I really missed him. Missed them. Missed everyone. But since Chloe was the only one around, I decided to vent my pain on her. "How long are you going to stay mad at me, Chloe? I know I've said this before, but what happened with Jake and me was a slow process. It's not like I got on that boat hoping to steal my sister's boyfriend."

"Are you sure?" Chloe said, leaning forward, fire in her eyes. "Because now I'm replaying that night at the sports bar. You know, when you were all over Jake all night long. You went home with him, Valerie."

Shame flooded me. "I did *not* go home with him. We shared a cab, but nothing happened. Nothing happened until the island, and even then, nothing happened until we were both pretty sure we'd never make it off the island." Chloe pursed her lips, but she didn't argue. "Okay, yes," I sighed. "I was attracted to him, and maybe we flirted a little too much that night, but I resisted him for as long as I could because I didn't want to hurt my sister. What would you have done differently if you were in my place?"

Alicia snorted. "I would have screwed him the first night on the island."

Remembering the sunburn, the bugbites, and the severe hunger, I really doubted she would have, but I smiled at her comment anyway. "Thanks for understanding, Alicia."

Steph nodded as she looked Chloe's way. "She really did try, Chloe. And as I always say, it takes two. Jake is just as much to blame as Valerie. But really, neither one of them meant to fall in love. Might as well blame the boat for sinking."

Chloe's eyes widened in surprise. "Fall in love? Kylie never mentioned love. She made it seem very . . . sordid."

My eyes brimmed with tears as I thought about everything Jake and I had gone through, as well as everything we had then sacrificed in the hopes that Kylie and I could somehow reclaim our friendship. But our plan wasn't working. I missed him so much it hurt, and Kylie still hated me. "Yes, we were very much in love . . . but I think it's easier for Kylie to think of it as something . . . dirty. She can freely hate me instead of trying to understand."

Chloe frowned. "That's not right. I mean . . . maybe what you did wasn't right, either, but if you fell for each other, and you thought you were stuck there . . ." She let out a long sigh. "I forgive you, Val. Even if she can't, I forgive you."

I started crying after that, then stood up and hugged Chloe. It wasn't until that very moment that I realized just how important her forgiveness was to me. And how important my sister's forgiveness was. It was time to stop letting her ignore me. It was time for a one-on-one with Kylie so that at the very least I could explain my side of things to her.

After saying good night to Steph, Alicia, and Chloe and after giving Alicia another enormous hug for her birthday, I hopped in a cab and made my way to Kylie's apartment. I began to worry about my sister along the way. Kylie had been devastated upon hearing about Jake's and my deaths, and then Jake and I had broken her heart—again. I should have ignored my own pain and gone to see her days ago. She was the entire reason Jake and I had split up. I should have confronted her back then, shouldn't have left her alone, suffering with no one. What if she had relapsed into another depression? What was I going to find when I knocked on her door?

Trepidation in my heart, I paid the cab driver—with money Dad had graciously given me for the evening—and headed to Kylie's apartment. I knocked, then waited. Nothing. It was late, though; she could be sleeping. I should probably come back in the morning. Stubbornness wouldn't let me back down, though. I needed to know that she was okay. I also needed her to understand and forgive me.

"Kylie?" I said, knocking a little louder. Still nothing. Frowning, I banged on the door. I didn't want to wake her neighbors, but I was a hairsbreadth away from knocking the door down. "Kylie?" I said even louder.

Finally, I heard movement inside and Kylie murmuring, "Hold on." I patiently waited while she slid the bolt and unlocked the door. When she saw it was me, she instantly started closing the door.

"Kylie, wait," I said, holding the door open with my foot.

Kylie let out a groan, then released her hold on the door. As she walked away, I walked inside. "What do you want, Valerie?" She twisted to look at me. "On second thought, don't answer that. I have nothing to say to you, and I don't care what you want to say to me."

The look on her face made my heart clench with pain. "Kylie, come on. At least hear me out."

Shaking her head, she walked over to her couch. I glanced around the room as I followed her. Her place was neat and tidy. Not a trace of take-out boxes, no wineglasses left around, no piles of dirty clothes lying about. It was just one room, but it spoke of someone who still cared about life. That was promising.

Kylie sat on the couch, then plopped her legs out sideways, blocking me from sitting next to her. Understandable. I took a chair kitty-corner to her instead. Scowling at me, she said, "I can't believe you're here, in my home, acting like we're still family."

"We are still family," I said.

Her eyes turned fiery. "Not anymore. Not since you slept with my boyfriend. Not since you stole him from me."

"I didn't," I said. "I let him go."

Shock stunned her into silence. Finally, she said, "What? Haven't you two been together since, well, the island?"

I cringed, then told her the truth. "For the first week, yes, we were together. But then he talked to you, and you were so upset. We were both so . . . we decided to not be together, since it hurt you so much. We decided to break it off and go our separate ways."

"For me," she murmured. "You gave him up . . . for me?"

Tears stung my eyes again. I had a feeling they always would when I thought about him. "Yes. I'd do anything for you, Kylie. I've always tried to put you first. Sometimes I failed, but I always tried. I love you."

Her mouth dropped open, and she stared at me, dumbfounded.

After a moment of silence, I asked her, "Can I please explain what happened now? Will you at least hear me out?"

Anger returned to her expression, but she simply nodded in answer.

My gut churned with guilt, but there was no going back now. "When we were on the island, we depended on each other to survive. There was no other way. Eventually, we grew . . . fond of each other. But we still kept our distance because of you. But over time we truly began to feel how deeply the odds were stacked against us, and we started to see that we were probably going to be stuck there forever. After accepting that, continuing to deny ourselves seemed . . . pointless."

That word riled my sister. "Pointless?" she hissed. "Respecting our relationship seemed pointless? And what about before the island? Chloe told me about that night at the sports bar. She said the two of you were all over each other. She said looking back on it, she was sure you slept with him that night. Did you?"

I let out a heavy sigh, which probably made me look guilty. And maybe I was. I should have restrained myself a little harder that night. I should have told Kylie way back then what I'd been feeling . . . what had happened. "No," I told her. "I didn't sleep with him. But we shared a cab, and yes . . . there was an attraction between us, but nothing happened other than a few soft words and tender touches."

She pressed her lips together, and her cheeks turned a bright red. "Soft words and tender touches? Jesus, Val. Is that supposed to make me feel better?"

Frustration grew in me, but I bit it back. She had a right to be angry. "I tried to do the right thing by you, Kylie. I met him at a coffee shop just a little bit after you started dating him. There was an instant spark between us, and I asked him out. But he said no, because he'd just started seeing someone. Then he showed up at family dinner . . . with you, his new girlfriend. The sparks were still there, but he was with you, so I did nothing. I did nothing until both of us genuinely felt like leaving that island was virtually impossible."

"And then you did do something."

"And then I did," I confirmed with a sigh. "And my entire world turned upside down. I lost you; I lost him; I lost everything."

"And was it worth it?" she asked, a pale eyebrow raised.

As I closed my eyes, a tear leaked out. "Hurting you was the last thing I ever wanted to do, and I'll never truly forgive myself for causing you so much pain, but . . . for that brief moment that we were together . . . yes." As I opened my eyes, a stuttered exhale escaped me; I felt like I was about to start sobbing, my chest hurt, and my throat was raw with grief. "Even now that he's gone, the memory of our time together is something I'll cherish for all my life."

Kylie's eyes widened at hearing the passion in my voice. "You really do love him, don't you?"

Sniffling, I nodded. "I do, and I know you do too. There's no winner here, only losers."

Kylie was silent a moment as she watched me struggle to rein in my feelings. Then she quietly said, "I understand. I'm not saying it doesn't hurt, I'm not saying you and I are instantly fine and all is forgiven, but . . . I understand."

A sad smile stretched across my lips. "That's all I can ask for." Reaching over, I put a hand on her arm. "I am truly sorry, Kylie. I never wanted a man to come between us. I never wanted anyone to come between us. We're . . . family."

Her chin wobbled as emotion flooded her. Then she rocketed off the couch and tossed her arms around me. "I love you, Val. You killed me, but I still love you."

I clenched her back just as fiercely as she was clinging to me. "I'm sorry, Kylie. I love you too. Please tell me you're okay. Please tell me you're going to be okay."

Kylie let out a sob as she held me. "You're alive. You're both alive. Even if Jake and I aren't together, even if things between you and I are strained . . . you're alive." She pulled back to look at me. "As long as you're alive, I'll be fine."

I grinned, then pulled her back to me for a hug. We cried together for a moment, then separated, Kylie returning to the couch, me sitting back in my chair. As we sat there sniffling, rubbing our eyes dry, an unsolved problem nagged at me. "Kylie . . . we should talk about Jake. I gave him up to mend things with you, but I still love him. We *both* still love him," I said, acknowledging her pain. "Jake is gone from my life, and he and I, we agreed to never talk again, but . . ." I paused as nerves washed through me. "I don't want there to be a problem between you and me again, but I still . . . want him. I want to be with him."

Kylie sighed, then said, "Val, I can't just . . . forget it all and give you my blessing."

Despair filled me, but I lowered my head and nodded. "I understand. I'll stay away from him."

Kylie sighed again. "I'm sorry if that seems petty. And I think a part of me knows that logically, I shouldn't be mad at you in the first place." She patted the spot beside her, and I joined her on the couch. Holding my hand, she softly said, "The second you and Jake 'died' . . . our relationship ended. We were already broken up when you got together. As broken up as a couple can get. And even if I'd hoped there was still a chance for us when he came back . . . I think I knew we were still broken up. Death just has a way of changing things."

I laughed, then squeezed her hand. "That is definitely true. And just so you know, he mourned you. He knew it was over. He knew you would move on once you believed he was dead, and that knowledge was really hard for him." It hurt to say it, but she needed to know how he felt.

Kylie smiled as she studied me. "That's pretty amazing of you to admit that." Then she frowned. "But it still hurts, and I just can't . . . if you really want to fix us, you need to stay away from him. I'm sorry . . . that might be wrong of me, but it's the truth."

My lip trembled as I shook my head. "All I can ask of you is to be honest with me. It's okay."

Kylie looked sad as she watched me. "So what are you going to do now?"

I slowly shook my head. "I'm going to let him go and focus on you and me . . . and my dream." Yes, that was how I'd get over him. Work. A small smile crept onto my lips. "I'm going to forget the past and focus on my future. You watch: this time next year, I'm going to be running my own restaurant."

She grinned as she leaned into my side. "I believe it." Straightening her back, she told me, "And a year from now, I'm going to be a successful artist. Maybe you'll even have my art on your walls."

"You bet your ass I will," I told her. We both laughed, and then I leaned my head against hers. "Thank you for letting me back in."

I felt her nod beneath me. "I already lost you once. I don't want to lose you again."

I smiled at her answer, but even still, a part of me was dying. To save what I had with Kylie, I had to give up the one person who felt like they'd been made for me. My soul mate.

Chapter Eighteen

Days passed. Then weeks. I was honoring my sister's wishes by staying away from Jake—not calling him, not going over to see him. He was doing his part, too, and staying away from me. It was torture, and I missed him every second of every day. But I wasn't wallowing in the pain. I had plans. Big plans.

Since I knew I couldn't live with my parents for the rest of my life, my first task had been to find a job. And since I was still relatively fresh from culinary school—and a touch famous after surviving a sinking boat—I'd landed a job as a sous chef at one of LA's poshest restaurants. It was *the* greatest place to work, and every day, I was learning more and more about what I needed to do for my own restaurant. But I did have to put up with a couple of minor annoyances . . .

"So tell me again how this guy pulled you from the water, saving your life."

I rolled my eyes as I glared at my coworker Phillipe. "There's nothing new to tell. Everything was covered in the interview."

He frowned as he stared at me. "But the *guy*, Valerie. You were on an island with him for months. You admitted to falling in love with him, having this epic romance, and then you come back here, and you just . . . split? That makes no sense . . ."

"Sorry to disappoint, but that's what happened." We'd sacrificed our love for the greater good. At least, that was what I kept telling myself.

Phillipe's frown deepened as he went back to making lobster ravioli for tonight's special. "That's just . . . lame. Where's the story, the drama, the romance? The happily ever after?"

I resisted the urge to toss my spoon at his face. "Real life doesn't always have those things, Phillipe."

"Maybe, maybe not, but still . . . it would be a much better story if you'd ended up with him."

Internally, I sighed. I'd believed that, too, at one point.

The head chef came in after that, silencing all conversations. I was grateful for the distraction. I was tired of talking about the island. Yes, it had happened; yes, parts of it had been good—really good—but a lot of it had been terrifying, and I was glad it was over with.

Chef Rourke started barking to Phillipe about the lack of uniformity in his ravioli, and I hid my smile. Chef reminded me a lot of Chef Sinclair. God, I missed that gruff man. His lifeless eyes still haunted me sometimes. I really wished I'd been able to get to know him better. I really wished he'd lived. I wished they'd all lived. Now that the romantic entanglement of that tragedy was over with, I'd been thinking a lot lately about all the lives that had been lost. All of them had deserved so much better than the fate they'd received.

When Chef Rourke was done setting Phillipe straight, he headed my way. His stern eyes looked over my pastry puffs. He made a grunting sound, then moved on to yell at someone else. "Bitch," Phillipe murmured. "Do you ever do anything wrong?"

I smiled at Phillipe, but inside I was cataloging everything I'd done wrong. It was a long list.

After my shift was over, I said goodbye to Phillipe and my other coworkers and headed to my car in the parking lot. Transportation had been my second priority. Third had been a tie between a place to live and a cell phone, both of which I'd successfully procured.

Climbing into my well-used but supercute coupe, I pulled out my phone and texted my sister. I'm on my way to the bar now. Are you still going out with us?

Yep, she said. See you there! Her text was littered with smiley faces, and I was happy to see them. One, it meant she truly wasn't mad at me, and two, it meant she was in a good mood. She'd been in a good mood a lot lately. I thought she'd finally recovered from losing Jake. I wanted to say the same thing about myself, but I wasn't sure if that was true. I still didn't sleep well. I still thought about him all the time. I still loved him.

Annoyed at myself, I tossed my phone into my bag and started the car. After way too many red lights, I finally pulled into the parking lot for the bar—the same sports bar that Jake and I had connected at so very long ago. I frowned as I looked over at the building that had been disastrous to me in so many ways, yet it had been wonderful too.

Walking into the bar, I quickly found my circle of friends: Steph, Alicia, Chloe, Kylie . . . and a strange man I'd never seen before. Kylie was giddy when she saw me, beaming from ear to ear. I tilted my head, studying her as I approached. And that was when it hit me—I'd seen her like this once before. She was in love. I shifted my eyes to her new love interest. He was about as different from Jake as you could get—dark eyes, dark hair, and just slightly taller than she was. Taken together as a couple, they were adorable.

"Hey," I said when I was close enough. "What's going on?"

Kylie giggled as she gave me a quick hug. "Val, I want you to meet my boyfriend, Simon."

I politely extended a hand, and Simon grabbed it. "It's nice to meet you," I told him. Releasing his hand, I turned back to my sister and added, "For the first time."

Kylie swished her hand at me. "I know it's the first time you've met. There's no way fate would do that to us twice. Plus, Simon is completely incapable of lying, and I already asked him about you."

Simon stuffed his hands in his pockets while his cheeks turned bright red. "Yeah, uh, never met, but I saw your interview a while ago. That was pretty crazy what you went through."

"You have no idea," I said, tossing on a smile.

Chloe patted the seat beside her, and I sat down with a grin. She gave me a quick squeeze around the shoulders. "Good to see you, Val. How's work?"

"Amazing," I told her, drawing out the word. "Chef Rourke is a bear, but I'm learning so much."

Steph and Alicia gave me bright smiles while Kylie and her boyfriend sat down. "We're so proud of you, Val," Steph said. "And you too, Kylie. We heard you're back at the beach doing caricatures and working on paintings that some have said are about to snatch top dollar."

Kylie raised an eyebrow. Simon grinned and kissed her cheek. "Who said that?" Kylie asked.

"Me," Alicia said. "And I know my shit."

Kylie rolled her eyes, but she was smiling brightly. It was so good to see her happy and to know she was doing well. It was almost enough to fill the aching hole in my heart. It made me wonder . . . maybe Kylie had moved on enough that she'd be okay if I contacted Jake. Or maybe that would be a trigger for her, reopening all the scars I'd caused and souring things between us again. I wanted to talk to her about it, but I was a little terrified of what she might say. And it probably didn't matter anyway. A guy like Jake didn't stay single long. *Stop thinking about him. It's long over, and he's not waiting around for you.*

Practicing forced awareness of the present, I pushed all thoughts of Jake from my mind. And that was when I heard Alicia say, "Damn . . . hot guy, twelve o'clock."

Her words brought a rush of pain through me. It hit me so hard I inadvertently inhaled a sharp breath. Kylie gently smacked Alicia across the arm. "Alicia, I doubt Simon wants a heads-up about some random hot guy."

Alicia laughed. "I didn't mention him for Simon's benefit. But there are three single girls at the table. Surely Simon doesn't mind if I help them out."

Laughing, Simon shook his head. "Go right ahead." Then he turned to face Kylie. "I'm all about people finding true love."

Alicia let out a loud groan as they kissed. "Get a room," she said, throwing a wadded napkin at them.

While Alicia laughed, Steph leaned back so she could look at the aforementioned hot guy. "Oooh, you're right, Alicia. He's . . . oh, isn't that . . ."

Her voice trailed off, and a sudden tension built up around the table. Oh no, it couldn't be . . . I closed my eyes, like somehow I could block out the truth. I wasn't ready to see him again; I didn't think I'd ever be ready.

I felt a hand on my shoulder. "Val," my sister said. "It's Jake. He's looking at you."

I held my breath as I slowly opened my eyes. She was right. Jake was sitting at the bar—just like that night—but this time he was twisted in his seat and was staring at our table. Staring at *me.*

My heart began to pound as our eyes locked. It had been so long since I'd seen him, and while he looked worn and tired, he was so attractive it hurt my heart. *God, I've missed you.* Jake's eyes were boring holes into me, and his expression was screaming that he wanted to come over and talk to me. I had no idea if he should.

I forced myself to break eye contact with him and look around the table. I half expected judgment from my friends, maybe resentment, but all of them—Kylie included—were giving me supportive smiles, like they wanted me to talk to him.

My gaze focused on Kylie. "We can leave. Go dancing or something."

Soft smile on her face, she shook her head. "It's okay, Valerie. I think you should go talk to him."

My eyes widened. "You do? Are you sure? I don't want to hurt you again."

Sitting back in her seat, Kylie grinned as she grabbed Simon's hand. "I'm positive, Valerie. I'm happy, truly happy, and I'm completely over him. But you're not. You've never stopped loving him, and I actually . . . feel really guilty for keeping you apart this long. So go talk to him. I'll only be angry with you if you don't."

I studied her face a moment, looking for any sign that she wasn't being completely honest. There was nothing but peace on her face, though, so I gave her a warm smile, then stood up and hugged her. Then I braced myself for a tidal wave of mixed emotions and started walking Jake's way.

Jake stood as he saw me approaching, and I could tell he was nervous. His eyes kept flicking between me and Kylie, and he almost looked like he wanted to run. When I was close enough, he started shaking his head. "I didn't know you were going to be here, I swear. I'm not trying to . . . I told you no contact, and I meant it. I wouldn't . . ."

He swallowed hard, and I could see the emotion written all over his face—the grief, the guilt, the desire. It welled up inside me, too, making my vision hazy and my throat tight. "I know," I told him. "I know you didn't plan this. We never planned any of this."

He cracked a tight smile at that. Then he looked down at my chest, and his smile grew. "You really do have the exact same shirt."

A small nervous laugh escaped me as I realized just what I was wearing. "Yeah . . . told you."

His smile dropped as he looked back at my sister. "Is Kylie . . . is she still mad at you? At us?"

There was a cringe on his face as he looked back at me. I inhaled a deep, calming breath. "No. She's . . . good." Some of my nerves evaporated as I said that, as I realized it was true. "She was angry for a long time, and even when she forgave me, she still didn't . . . she couldn't handle us being together. You were right about that. Separating was the only way to keep her in my life."

Jake nodded, his eyes drifting to the floor. "Well, I'm glad something good came out of all this."

Stepping forward, I grabbed his hands. He seemed shocked by the move, and his eyes snapped back to Kylie before returning to me. "I don't think . . . is this okay?" he asked, looking both confused and hopeful.

Touching him again made a rush of happiness course through me. It had been so long, and he felt so good. "I think so. She told me to talk to you. She . . . she wants this."

He still seemed floored, so much so that I began to worry. "Do you want this?" I asked. And it was only then that I realized . . . he might not want me back. Like my sister, he might have moved on. "Are you here with someone?" I asked, my heart pounding in my chest.

Jake slowly shook his head. Knowing my question wasn't truly a complete picture of his life, I said, "Do you have someone at home? Are you involved?"

Jake closed his eyes, and pain abolished all of my happiness. He wasn't single. We'd gone through all this, sacrificed all this, and he *still* wasn't single. I started pulling away from him, and Jake's eyes snapped open. He grabbed my hands, holding me in place. "No, I'm not involved. I'm not seeing anyone. I'm completely alone."

I bunched my brows, trying to understand. "Then why did you look so . . . I don't know, sad?"

A small smile touched his lips. "Because I've been having this dream every night since I left your house, and for a split second there, I was positive that's all this was . . . just another dream. I knew I was about to wake up, about to start another day without you, and I just . . . I can't. I can't do it anymore, Valerie."

My heart surged with adrenaline and happiness. "You're single. I'm single. And my sister is finally happy again. Does that mean . . . ? Can we really . . . ?"

The hope was so fragile inside me that I couldn't even finish my questions. Jake pressed my hand against his chest, against his heart. "You're always with me, Val. And if you want me, I'm yours."

I did. Desperately. But I didn't want to ruin everything Kylie and I had rebuilt. I couldn't break up with Jake again if she wasn't truly on board—I wouldn't survive another forced separation. I opened my mouth to answer him, but no words came out. His worried eyes searched my face, and then, at the same time, we both twisted to look at my sister.

She was still sitting at the table with my friends, and all of them were relentlessly staring at us. Heat started rushing to my cheeks at being under their intense scrutiny, but I ignored the sensation and focused on Kylie. She was the only one I cared about at the moment. She stared back at me, her blue eyes bright, her smile dazzling. Simon had his arm around her shoulders, and he was watching the exchange with curious—but unworried—eyes.

Finally, after an eternity that was probably only a few seconds, Kylie cupped her hands to her mouth and shouted, "Kiss her, you idiot!"

I frowned at her calling Jake an idiot, then turned back to him with a smile on my face. I was about to tell him yes, I wanted him, when his lips crashed down to mine. The bar instantly filled with hooting and hollering, but the sound was drowned out by my rampaging heart. His mouth on mine again was like a jolt to my soul, revitalizing my spirit, filling me with life and hope. I felt like anything was possible again.

When we finally broke apart, we were both breathless. Feeling almost delirious with joy, I laced my arms around his neck and told him, "I want you. Today, tomorrow . . . forever, I want you."

His grin was infectious, and then his smile softened, his hand cupped my cheek, and his thumb began tenderly stroking the skin. A bittersweet memory rushed over me: *You're so beautiful.* He'd always seen me as more than he could ever confess to my sister. He'd loved me from the beginning, and that love had only grown on the island. And then he'd done the unthinkable . . . he'd let me go to save my family from falling apart. How many guys would do that? Be that selfless? None that I had ever met. He was one of a kind, made just for me, and now, finally, we could actually be together.

"I love you," I whispered, feeling like my heart might beat its way out of my chest.

Jake smiled. "I love you too," he said, and then he leaned forward and placed his lips against mine, gently this time. And for the first time in a long time, I felt the void inside me completely fill. God, I'd missed him.

Chapter Nineteen

I could not believe what was happening today. One year and three months after telling my sister I would do it, I'd actually done it. My dream fulfilled, my greatest desire completed. Tomorrow was the grand opening of my restaurant. *My* restaurant. Just thinking about it made me want to pinch myself. In fact, I had already done that about ten times today.

The grin on my face was frozen in place as I put on my chef's jacket. I'd had the same expression plastered on me ever since the bank had approved my loan. It was happening!

Arms wrapped around me from behind, and soft lips nuzzled my ear. "You're going to wear that all night long, aren't you?"

Giggling, I relaxed into Jake's arms. "You bet your ass I am, Captain." A few months ago, Jake had taken a job captaining a charter boat for sports fishermen. It was small compared to the cruise ship he'd originally dreamed of captaining, but as it turned out—he absolutely loved it. And I loved the fact that he was home every evening, not out on the open ocean. "I might even sleep in it," I told him.

His lips drifted to my neck. "We'll see about that," he murmured.

I laughed, then twisted in his arms. "Can you believe it, Jake? Isla Bonita is finally about to open."

He grinned, his beautiful jade eyes sparkling with love and contentment. "I love the name you chose. All I can think about is you when I hear it."

"Yeah," I said, looping my arms around his neck. "It reminds me of you too. Of everything we went through . . . everything we lost . . . and gained." I felt tears stinging my eyes, and I laughed again as I wiped them dry. "I don't know why I'm such a wreck. I've been crying at the drop of a hat lately."

"That's joy, Valerie. Joy of finally seeing something you've been . . . craving . . . become yours. I know that feeling well," he whispered. He leaned down to kiss me, and every nerve ending tingled.

I pulled him in tighter, deepening our kiss, our connection. It had taken me a while to fully give my heart to Jake again. At first, after we'd reconnected, I'd kept a piece of my soul in a tiny box, worried that something would tear us apart again. But nothing bad had happened, and time had slowly chipped away the walls until there was nothing left. I was laid bare before him—a terrifying but intoxicating feeling.

Jake's hands moved up my back to my shoulders, and I could feel him removing my jacket. My new, embroidered Isla Bonita jacket. I smacked his fingers away, then told him, "The jacket stays on, mister."

He grinned, then nodded. "Yes, ma'am." He left the jacket alone, removing my jeans instead. As I laughed, my joy infecting every part of me, Jake stripped the clothes that I allowed him to strip. When I was mostly bare—just my unbuttoned jacket remaining—he laid me on my bed. *Our* bed. We'd officially moved in together two months ago, after I'd finally relented to his ceaseless insistence that him coming over every night practically constituted living together anyway.

And living with him . . . it reminded me so much of the island, of falling in love with him. Every night that I fell asleep by his side was another night that I felt wholly and completely at peace. I'd never imagined that being in a relationship *like this* would be so . . . fulfilling.

Jake kissed up my thighs, savoring every inch of me. I closed my eyes, enjoying his ministrations. His lips traveled up my abdomen, then between my breasts. He lingered over my nipple, circling with his tongue around it before sucking it into his mouth. I let out a satisfied groan as familiar desire ran through me; it never ceased to amaze me how easily he could turn me on.

I pulled his mouth up to mine, then ran my hands to his jeans. Unfastening them, I ran my hand down the length of him. He was completely ready for me. Already. I wasn't the only one who was easily turned on. Jake groaned under my ministrations, then ripped his clothes off as quickly as humanly possible.

I giggled when he returned to my side, then moved over on top of him. I rubbed against him, letting him feel how much I wanted him. I teased us both, letting the desire surge and grow, escalating into something glorious. Our breaths grew fast, our heartbeats quickened, and just when I was so ready I couldn't take any more, Jake flipped me over to my back. He gently pushed into me, savoring every inch of our connection. When he was as deep as he could go, he paused. Desire surged in me to the point where I felt like I was about to burst. Like he could read my mind, he finally began to move.

With my jacket splayed on the mattress around me, the euphoria began rising within me. I held Jake tight, wanting to experience every second of it with him. Our movements became more frantic, our breaths heavier, faster. I could feel the ecstasy cresting, almost within reach. And then it was there, exploding over me in a tidal wave of bliss.

I clenched Jake's shoulders, digging in with my nails as the moment intensified. As I pressed in, Jake cried out, and then I felt his own release. I savored the moment as I came down off my own high. God, I loved making love to this man. And knowing we could do it without guilt made it all the better. Actually, it made it a million times better.

We lay there for a moment, panting, reclaiming our breaths. When we were both calm and mellow, Jake gave me a soft kiss, then moved to my side. He fingered a button on my jacket, a soft smile on his face. "I like this. I think you should wear it every time."

I laughed at his comment, then sighed with contentment. "Do you think everything will go okay tomorrow?"

"I know it will. It will be more than fine. It will be great." Grabbing my cheeks, he stared me right in the eyes. "You've prepared, you've learned, you've planned, you've advertised the hell out of it . . . there's no way tomorrow won't be amazing."

Biting my lip, I tried to contain my grin. I couldn't. "I'm too excited to sleep. Make me forget about time so tomorrow comes faster."

Jake smiled, then softly kissed me. "Yes, ma'am," he said, running his hand over my breast.

And then he did his best to make sure that I forgot all about the time.

~

The next morning, I was nervous, anxious, and more excited than I'd ever been in all my life. Today was the day! In just a handful of hours, Isla Bonita would be opening its doors for the first time. I was so giddy. I jumped out of bed and into the shower. Jake tried to join me, but I shooed him out. Last night had been our fun night; today, I needed to focus.

After showering, Jake and I immediately headed for the restaurant. I couldn't believe how lucky I'd gotten with the location; it was in the perfect spot, right in the heart of the historic theater district. Every restaurant that had been here before had done really well. The only reason the building was even available was because the previous restaurant's owners had decided to sell and retire. I'd scooped it up and completely revamped it to match my style. It was everything I'd always wanted. Kind of like Jake.

Unlocking the restaurant made me giddy. Stepping inside took my breath away—every single time. The entire space had a cozy, intimate, stranded-on-a-tropical-island feel to it. But it was done in a really classy way, with tall vases full of tropical flowers tucked in every corner, luxurious velvet chairs surrounding every white-linen-covered table, and exquisite art decorating every wall. My sister's art. Over the last year, she'd really perfected her skill, and all the walls were covered with various island scenes. They were all so real, so exceptional—particularly this one of a pristine bay—that it was almost like Kylie had been with us on that abandoned island. And in a way, maybe she had been.

Holding hands with Jake, I walked into the kitchen. The menu for the restaurant had been the real challenge. Seafood seemed the natural choice with the island theme, but then I'd decided to round it out with beef and chicken. A little something for everyone. All of the food was top notch and high quality. That made the restaurant a little on the higher-priced side, but everyone I'd spoken to had assured me people would gladly pay the price to eat my food. I certainly hoped so; otherwise Isla Bonita might be the first failure in this location.

Everything in the kitchen was still bright, shiny, and new. It made me want to dirty things up. "So," Jake said, "where would you like me?" I cocked an eyebrow at him. He did look amazing in his tailored suit, but we didn't have time for that right now. Jake smiled. "For work. What would you like me to do?"

I laughed at his comment, then grinned. "We need to chop . . . everything."

Jake groaned—he didn't have my speed, so he hated cutting things up around me. He said it was emasculating. I said he just needed practice, so I made him cut up a *lot* of stuff.

The rest of the staff arrived while we were working. Phillipe smiled at me, then took over what I was chopping. "You're the boss," he said. "Let your minions do your prep work."

I frowned as he pushed me back a step. "You're not my minion, Phillipe. You're still my coworker."

He grinned at me over his shoulder. "So we can go grab a beer and bitch about the boss?"

"Of course. Anytime you want to." I paused to point a stern finger at him. "After your shift."

I'd poached Phillipe and a couple of other cooks from my old job with Chef Rourke. It had taken a lot of faith in me for them to leave that cushy job for this new venture, and I really hoped I didn't let them down.

As I left Phillipe and the others to their work, I double-checked that everything was ready for the opening. Wine chilled, silverware cleaned, linens spotless, chairs smoothed, flowers watered, lights dimmed . . . we were all set. Inhaling a deep breath, I unlocked the front doors. *Come on in, world. I'm ready for you.*

Jake rubbed my back while I stood there, absorbing the moment. Twisting around, I smiled at him, then looked past him to the hostess. "When's the first reservation?"

Her hair and outfit immaculate, she gave me a bright, model-worthy smile. "In twenty minutes. Then we're booked for most of the entire night."

I nodded as I let out an anxiety-ridden exhale. "Good . . . that's good . . ." Nerves began to eat at my enthusiasm. What if people canceled? What if no one showed up? I knew that was highly improbable, but still . . .

Jake turned me around to look at him. "Hey, it's going to be all right. You've got this," he added with a grin.

Remembering saying those words to him on the island made me grin. "Yes. Yes, I do." I practically skipped my way back to the kitchen.

Throughout the night Jake became my eyes into the dining room as I worked my ass off in the kitchen. "Table number one seems very happy with their meal. And with the waitress. You did a great job hiring her. She's extremely knowledgeable but funny and relatable too. People like that combination." He closed the kitchen door to look at me. "I knew you'd be a natural at this."

I grinned at him, then threw Phillipe a quick smile. She had been his suggestion.

Jake cracked the door open again as he continued spying on our patrons. "Table five just sat down. That guy looks like a beef guy to me . . . and a big spender. Wagyu. His date seems more reserved. Salmon, for sure."

I laughed at his assessment, but damn if he wasn't spot on. If Jake weren't completely happy with his job, I would have hired him on as a manager or something.

The night continued on, and I was shocked at how busy we were. Not all of the tables had been reserved, and that meant we were getting walk-ins. That was huge for us. Even though we were an upscale place, we would still need to rely on the drop-ins for long-term success.

About halfway through the night, Jake turned to me with a wide smile on his face. "Val, you have VIPs at table twelve. You're going to have to take a break and greet them yourself."

I looked at him with wide, incredulous eyes. "Are you serious? I'm a mess right now." To emphasize my point, I pointed at my hair—discreetly tied up in a clear hairnet—and the sweat dripping down the side of my neck.

Jake's grin grew. "You're beautiful," he told me, and damn if those two words didn't make my heart flutter.

"Fine," I sputtered, still smiling. "Take over, Phillipe. I guess I've got to meet some VIPs."

"All part of being the boss, boss."

I rolled my eyes at Phillipe, then dried my hands and my face and made my way to the door. Jake held it open for me, a secretive smile on his face. I walked into the heart of the dining room and took a look around. Damn. It was packed in here, but everyone looked . . . happy, satisfied, content. The people eating their food were closing their eyes, savoring it. The people waiting for food were sipping on drinks, chatting quietly with each other. Seeing the people so happy at my place, eating my food, made my eyes burn with tears. I felt the tightening of a sob begin to form, but I swallowed it back. The owner of the restaurant having an emotional meltdown on opening night wasn't the headline I wanted to be reading in the morning.

"This way," Jake said, grabbing my elbow.

I had no idea who the VIPs were Jake wanted me to greet, but the mystery didn't last long. When we arrived at a large table within eyesight of the kitchen door, I was nearly overcome with surprise. "Mom, Dad . . . Steph, Alicia . . . Chloe, Kylie . . . Simon?"

Even though this was their special table—with their names engraved on a plaque that sat on top of it—none of them had mentioned coming out tonight. My family and I had planned on all having dinner together sometime next week, when the craziness of the grand opening had died down. Seeing them all here—together—was too much for my joy-heavy heart.

"Oh my God, you guys." Tears began streaming down my face, and I hastily wiped them away. "I can't believe you're . . . oh my God . . ."

My mom swiped her eyes as she moved forward to hug me. "Did you really think we'd miss your opening night?"

"Yes," I said, half sobbing. "We had plans."

"Plans change," Kylie said. She gave Jake a knowing smirk as she rose from the table. It took her a moment to stand with the massive baby bump she was sporting. Her husband, Simon, gave her a hand, and she gleefully walked into my arms. "This is amazing, Val. Absolutely amazing."

Feeling the life between us kick and move in her belly, I laughed and put a hand on her stomach. "No, this is amazing. And your art. I think you're going to get a ton of inquiries." All of her art on the walls had her name and the address and phone number of her art studio on a placard beneath it. Just in my brief time in the dining room, I'd seen a half dozen people pointing and commenting on her work. My success was going to be her success; I was sure of it.

Kylie giggled and crossed her fingers. "Here's hoping."

Simon squeezed her shoulder. "No, she's right; I can tell. This is going to be big for you. Both of you. Congratulations, Valerie."

"Thank you, Simon," I said, grinning at my brother-in-law.

When Kylie and I finally separated, Jake moved forward. Smiling warmly at her, he said, "You look great, Kylie. How much longer do you have to go?"

Kylie groaned as she grabbed her stomach with both hands. "Would you believe I still have two more freaking months?" She gave Simon a weary expression. "I'm going to be the size of a house."

Simon grinned wider. "And I'll love every inch of you."

Jake laughed, then looked at me with longing in his eyes. We hadn't discussed kids yet or even seriously talked about marriage. I had a feeling both of those conversations were fast approaching.

Dad hugged me, congratulating me; then Alicia and Chloe took their turns. Steph waited until last. Her eyes were misty when she finally approached me. "You're wearing a hairnet," she said.

I knocked her shoulder back as I rolled my eyes. "Thanks for noticing."

She laughed, then tossed her arms around me. "I'm so proud of you, Val. This place . . . it's truly one of a kind." Pulling back, she looked between Jake and me. "Honestly, if what happened with you two hadn't happened, none of *this* would have happened." She looked back at Kylie, including my radiant sister in her assessment.

With a happy sigh, I leaned into Jake's side. "Yeah, I know." Jake and I had always been interested in each other, but without that trauma, that life-changing event, we might have only pined over each other from afar.

"I should probably get back to the kitchen," I said, wiping my eyes for the millionth time. Everyone said their goodbyes with one final round of hugs. Pointing at them, I said, "I'm going to make you the best meal you've ever had."

Mom and Dad smiled, pride on their faces, and I went back to the kitchen feeling a renewed sense of vigor and determination. Like Jake said, *I've got this.*

I paid extra-special attention to my family's and friends' meals, personally overseeing every aspect. While they ate their food, Jake gave me a play-by-play of their reactions. All of it was positive. When they were finished and ready to leave, they stepped into the kitchen to say their goodbyes, swearing it was legitimately the best food they'd ever tasted. After they were gone, the rest of the night flew by faster than seemed possible. I was exhausted by the time the evening was over.

Once all the customers and staff were gone, it was just Jake and me in the kitchen, unwinding with a glass of wine. I suddenly felt every ache and pain that I had earned today, and I was dreaming of a nice, hot bath. Jake had other plans, though.

Walking over, he held a hand out to me. "I want to show you something."

I tilted my head, confused and curious. "Show me what?" I asked, grabbing his hand.

"You'll see," he said, leading me into the dining room.

Shaking my head, I let him lead me to a small table in the corner. It was set up with a pair of tall candles and covered plates. Tilting my head again, I looked over at him. "What's all this?"

He shrugged. "I happened to notice that you haven't eaten all day. This exquisitely prepared meal is for you."

My eyes were wide as I stared at the dishes. "When? How?"

A small laugh escaped him. "That last-minute order might have come from me."

Warmth spread through my chest and my heart as I studied him. "Have I told you recently how amazing you are?"

Pursing his lips, he tilted his head. "Maybe a couple of times last night, but no, not today."

I grinned at him, then wrapped my arms around his neck. "Well, you are. You're absolutely amazing."

He gave me a soft kiss and murmured, "I'm not the only one. You were outstanding today, but you didn't eat. And I believe we made a pact that we wouldn't go another day without eating."

I smirked as I moved away from him. "I don't recall a pact . . . but okay, I'll eat. I'm actually starving, so this is perfect."

"I know," he said, pulling out my chair.

His chivalry made me feel those butterflies. Funny how some things never went away. Sitting down, I let him push me slightly under the table. "So what did you order for me?" I asked. "I was on autopilot, and I don't remember what the last order was for . . ."

All speech left me as Jake pulled off the cover on my plate and I saw what he'd prepared for me. It was my signature dish, a perfectly cooked lobster, but sitting on top of the bright-red shell was a tiny, unmistakable box. My heart raced as I stared at it. "Oh . . . God . . ."

Jake picked up the small box. My eyes tracked his every movement, and when he began to sink onto one knee, the tears were instant and unstoppable. "Valerie, I—"

"Yes!" I exclaimed, starting to sob.

Jake frowned. "I haven't asked you yet."

A laughing cry left my lips. "Well, will you hurry up and ask me so I can say yes?"

Jake laughed, then nodded. "Valerie, I love you more than I thought it possible to love someone. Will you do me the honor of marrying me?"

He opened the box, exposing a beautiful solitaire diamond on a silver band. Not answering him, I leaped out of my chair, tossed my arms around him, and immediately found his mouth. Our kiss was soft, sweet, and full of tears. Finally, Jake pulled back to look at me. "It's still a yes, right?"

I laughed, then nodded. "Yes. It's always been a yes." I cupped his cheek with my hand, softly stroking his stubbled skin. "From day one I've wanted to be with you, freely, clearly, no guilt or remorse. From day one, I've loved you."

He smiled as he stared at me. "From day one, I've loved you too. I just didn't know it, but now that I do, it's so obvious to me . . . you're my soul mate, and I want to spend the rest of my life with you."

And now we could. Now there was nothing holding us back, nothing keeping us apart, nothing stopping our dreams from coming true. Everything was exactly how I'd always wanted it to be, and then some. I never could have imagined, way back in the beginning, that my life would turn out so . . . perfect.

ACKNOWLEDGMENTS

I would like to thank all the readers who have been so supportive of me over the years. Your never-ending love for my characters means the world to me. A huge thank-you to everyone who reached out to me with praise for my last book, *Under the Northern Lights*. That one was a little different for me and very special, and I'm so glad it resonated with so many of you.

Thank you to my superagent, Kristyn Benton of ICM Partners. As always, your calming words were just what I needed to hear. Thank you to everyone at Montlake / Amazon Publishing. I love being a part of the Amazon family, and you have all been so wonderful to work with. A special thank-you to Lindsey Faber—your help was invaluable—and Lauren Plude: your cheerful support is so appreciated.

And lastly, thank you to my friends and my family. Thank you for listening to my woes, trying to make me feel better when nothing is working out, and celebrating all the little victories with me. Love you all! I am truly blessed.

ACKNOWLEDGMENTS

ABOUT THE AUTHOR

Photo © Tarra Ellis Photography

S.C. Stephens is a bestselling author who enjoys spending every free moment creating stories that are packed with emotion and heavy on romance. Her debut novel, *Thoughtless*, an angst-filled love story featuring insurmountable passion and the unforgettable Kellan Kyle, took the world of romance by storm in 2009. Stephens has been writing nonstop ever since.

In addition to writing, Stephens enjoys spending lazy afternoons in the sun reading fabulous novels, loading up her iPod with writer's block–reducing music, heading out to the movies, and spending quality time with her friends and family. She currently resides in the beautiful Pacific Northwest with her two equally beautiful children.